# Some Trust Can Be Rebuilt

Jane Blythe

Bear Spots Publications
Melbourne Australia

Paperback
ISBN-13: 978-0-6452796-0-3

Cover designed by QDesigns

SOME QUESTIONS HAVE NO ANSWERS
SOME TRUTH CAN BE DISTORTED
SOME TRUST CAN BE REBUILT

Saving SEALs Series

SAVING RYDER
SAVING ERIC
SAVING OWEN
SAVING LOGAN

Christmas Romantic Suspense Series

CHRISTMAS HOSTAGE
CHRISTMAS CAPTIVE
CHRISTMAS VICTIM
YULETIDE PROTECTOR

I'd like to thank everyone who played a part in bringing this story to life. Particularly my mom who is always there to share her thoughts and opinions with me. My awesome cover designer, Amy, who whips up covers for me so quickly and who patiently makes every change I ask for, and there are usually lots of them! And my lovely editor Lisa Edwards, for all their encouragement and for all the hard work they put into polishing my work.

# OCTOBER 4<sup>TH</sup>

8:04 P.M.

A twig snapped beneath her foot.

Mia Taylor flinched as the sound seemed exorbitantly loud in the otherwise quiet forest.

"Stop being silly," she reprimanded herself even as she spun in a slow circle checking out her surroundings, her eyes straining to see through the dark for whatever was making the hairs on the back of her neck stand out.

She really was being silly.

She knew that.

Mia was head of search and rescue in River's End and the surrounding area, and she had done hundreds—literally—of searches just like this one so she had no idea why tonight felt different. Something was making her feel on edge like someone was watching her, but nobody was there every time she turned around.

Ignoring the burning in her back like a pair of eyes were boring into her, she resumed walking. Determined to shove away the unsettling feeling of being watched, Mia knew she had more important things to worry about like finding ten-year-old Devin Deville. The child had gone missing nearly four hours ago on his walk home from school. He'd left the school with his friends, walked part of the way with them, then vanished into thin air.

Devin Deville had never made it home.

His backpack had been found about two miles from his house just on the outskirts of the forest.

1

That was when she and her team had been called in.

Mia had always hated looking for missing kids, especially when they were on their own, it brought back a lot of memories. She's been eight when she'd gotten lost while out playing with her friends. She had grown up in River's End, both of her parents had worked at the elementary school, and the forest had been an extension of her home. All the kids in town would spend hours out here, playing, fishing, and camping. During one game of hide and seek, she had been determined to win and wandered off to find the perfect place to hide, and soon realized she couldn't find her way back.

Those ten hours that she had been out there, alone and scared, had been imprinted on her soul and been the reason she had chosen this career. Those feelings, while she'd never forgotten them, had faded and been replaced by the adrenalin rush of finding someone lost or injured and bringing them safely home. Of course there were days where that didn't happen, where the person they were looking for had succumbed to an injury or the elements and returned to their family in a body bag.

Tonight those old feelings of fear and uneasiness were back, and she couldn't shake them no matter how hard she tried.

Was that how little Devin felt right now?

Since River's End was a small town where everybody knew everybody, Mia knew Devin. The kid was cute as could be and an amazing singer. Last year he'd sung during the annual Christmas party and had the entire town in tears. He was cheeky like most kids his age, but he was sweet, and she'd caught him a couple of weeks ago standing up for a younger child who was being teased even though he'd brushed off his involvement and said it was no big deal when she'd stepped in to help.

Now that great kid was lost out there somewhere. They had no idea why he'd come out here, he was a good kid who always went home straight after school, so there was always the possibility that he hadn't come into the forest of his own free will.

2

The thought made her shudder even though the night wasn't too cold.

If someone had abducted the boy, what would she see when he was found? Would he be hurt? Dead?

Was the abductor the one out here watching her and making her skin crawl?

Quickly Mia spun in a circle, searching for anything that moved that shouldn't be moving.

The forest was quiet, there was no breeze, and the sky was clear making dappled moonlight shine through the trees. The flashlight on her helmet lit up the way, and as she turned around slowly she made sure to check out each tree to ensure no one was hiding behind it.

"Stop it, Mia," she mumbled under her breath. She had to stop freaking herself out like this. She was just out in the forest, the place where she had grown up, the place where she worked, there was no reason to be so edgy. Maybe it was just because this was the first missing kid that she'd looked for in a while. And the fact that this was different than most of her cases. Most of the time, they were looking for hikers or campers who had wandered off and gotten lost or someone who had fallen and injured themselves. They didn't look for kids that might have been kidnapped.

All of his friends were accounted for so Devin hadn't run off to play with one of them. There were no reported problems at home or school so it didn't look like he had a reason to run away, which pretty much left kidnapping as the only viable explanation for the child's disappearance.

Could that really be what happened to Devin?

Forcing herself to stop compulsively checking her surroundings, Mia continued walking. They'd divided the forest into grids based on when the boy went missing and the maximum distance someone could cover in that time. The search team had been assembled and started out almost an hour ago, and she had covered roughly about half of her area so far. She had to keep going. If Devin was indeed out there then they had to find him.

Although the feeling that she wasn't alone out here didn't dwindle, Mia did her best to shake it off and continue her search. She had walked for about another five minutes when she saw something up ahead.

It was small and red.

Devin had been wearing a red sweater and jeans when he disappeared.

Was that him?

Although she wanted to run up to what could be the missing boy and make sure he was okay, she had to make sure it was safe to do so. As a first aid provider, she knew that the primary and most important thing she could do for any victim in her care was to make sure she stayed safe. If there was a problem and she ran headlong into it, then all they would have was two victims.

"Devin?" Mia called out. "Devin, it's search and rescue, it's me, Mia. If you can hear me, honey, I need you to let me know."

Nothing.

Checking the area out as she approached, she couldn't see anything that caused alarm, and a moment later she was crouching down beside the child. In the bright light from her helmet, the boy looked pale, but as she visually scanned his body she couldn't see any injuries.

He looked like he was asleep. Given that he hadn't woken up at her presence or when she called his name, she assumed he was unconscious and not actually sleeping.

What had happened to him?

He was fully clothed, and that was a relief she couldn't even put into words. If he was dressed she hoped that meant he hadn't been … touched … violated.

There were sticks and leaves in his hair and his hands were folded together and resting on his stomach. They had obviously been placed there which pretty much confirmed the idea that someone had brought him out here and left him.

Was that person still here?

Mia quickly looked around again as she reached for her radio to call in that she had found the boy.

Before she could call, she heard it.

Snapping twigs.

Footsteps.

Someone was coming.

Quickly she scanned the ground around where she was kneeling in search of a weapon. There were no predators out here, and she didn't carry a gun, but now she wished that she did. What was she going to do to protect herself and Devin if this was his abductor returning?

Realizing there was nothing she could use that would compete with a real weapon, Mia curled her fingers around the nearest rock and picked it up. She turned off her flashlight, no need to use a beacon to draw in Devin's attacker, and held her breath as she waited.

The footsteps got closer.

She could see a figure moving through the trees.

The shadowy figure was huge. Whoever was coming wasn't someone she was going to be able to fight off easily.

The weight of the rock in her hand comforted her a little. Her best bet was to throw it at him, hope it connected, then pick up the kid and hope she was big enough and strong enough to carry him out of here.

He got closer, and she lifted her arm, ready to throw her rock.

He stepped out from behind a tree and Mia didn't hesitate, just flung the rock as hard as she could.

As soon as she had she scrambled to grab ahold of Devin. She didn't have any time to waste.

"Ouch," the shadowy figure said as the rock obviously connected with her target.

Mia froze.

She knew that voice.

She just didn't know what it was doing out here.

"Julian?"

* * * * *

8:33 P.M.

Deputy Sheriff Julian Black winced as something hard connected with his shoulder.

"Ouch," he exclaimed, his hand immediately going to rub the sore spot. He'd joined the search for missing River's End resident ten-year-old Devin Deville, but about thirty minutes into searching the grid he had been assigned, the flashlight on his helmet had blinked out. Not wanting to go back without finishing his search he'd continued on, reasoning that there was enough light from the moon to see where he was going. When he'd seen a light up ahead of him, he'd headed straight for it only to have it blink out too.

"Julian?"

The voice startled him. Not because he thought he was alone out here, he knew from both the light and the fact that someone had thrown something at him that he wasn't, but because the voice belonged to the only woman he had ever loved.

The woman he had failed.

The woman he had been thinking more and more about these last couple of months.

"Mia?" he asked, taking a step toward the shadowy figures he could see crouched near the ground. Had she tripped and hurt herself? Was that why her light had suddenly gone out? "Are you okay?"

Her light turned back on, and he saw that she was kneeling beside the body of a boy. Devin Deville. "I'm okay, I found Devin, and then I saw someone walking around without a headlight. I didn't know it was you, I was worried it was whoever had taken Devin," she explained in a rush, sounding jittery and borderline scared, nothing like the calm, competent search and rescue expert he knew her to be.

Assuming she was just freaked out about the nature of the search—no one wanted to be looking for a potentially abducted child—he closed the distance between them and dropped down on the other side of the boy. "He alive?"

Mia nodded. "He has a pulse, but he's asleep. Well, not asleep, I think he's been drugged."

"Any injuries?"

"None that I could see."

So someone had abducted the kid, brought him out to the forest, drugged him but not physically assaulted him, and then just left him here and disappeared. That seemed, well, for lack of a better word, odd. Julian had served in the military before returning to the town where he had grown up and joined the local police department, he'd seen the worst atrocities that one human being could do to another. His mind screamed at him that there had to be more to it than that.

Sexual assault.

That was the most obvious answer.

Whoever had abducted Devin probably brought him out here where they wouldn't be interrupted, drugged the child to keep him compliant, did what they'd taken the kid to do, then left him out here.

That, or Mia had interrupted things before the kidnapper could kill the boy.

Unsettled by that thought, Julian quickly scanned their surroundings, his hand moving to hover above his gun.

Mia, observant thing that she was, noticed and immediately began to look around just like he was. "Do you see someone?" she hissed.

"No, just being cautious," he assured her. Mia already seemed wired tonight, and he didn't want to alarm her.

Conscious of the fact that this could be a crime scene, Julian weighed their options. Devin was unconscious, they didn't know what he had been given or the effects it would have on him, the priority had to be getting him to the hospital. Since the boy obviously hadn't done this to himself, they also had to think about preserving evidence. Mia had already touched the kid, and he'd be carrying Devin back to base so their clothes would have to be collected along with Devin's. Other than that, they would just have to pray that nothing—human, animal, or nature—messed with the site until a forensics team could get there.

"I'm going to take a few pictures. Why don't you set up some markers so CSU knows where to work?" he said as he pulled his phone from his back pocket. It wouldn't take great pictures in the dark, but it was better than nothing.

While Mia set up markers around Devin, Julian took his photos, then popped his phone away and wrapped the child in the Mylar blanket Mia had pulled from her pack before scooping him up. The boy was small and his weight wouldn't slow them down any on the trek back.

Mia had pulled out her radio once she'd finished marking the spot and called in to say that they had Devin and were heading back, and that all other search teams should also return to base. With a last lingering look around, she focused on him. "Ready to get out of here?"

"Absolutely," he agreed as he followed after her when she started walking. Julian couldn't not stare at her cute little backside as she navigated with ease through the forest. And since he couldn't not stare at her backside, he couldn't not remember how it felt in his hands when he'd lift her up, bury himself deep inside her, and come so hard he'd forget his own name.

Forget everything but her and how perfect she was.

It had been almost eighteen months since their relationship disintegrated and he hadn't forgotten a single thing about her. Not the way she scrunched up her nose when she was concentrating, or the way she took forever to eat her food, or the way she'd hum a moan when his mouth was devouring every part of her body. And he certainly hadn't forgotten how much he loved her and how much he regretted what had happened.

Losing Mia was the biggest regret of his life.

If he could take back everything that had happened two years ago he would in a heartbeat, but unfortunately, life didn't work that way.

You couldn't go back you could only keep going forward, and ever since his brother Will had reunited with his ex, and they had both managed to overcome the seemingly insurmountable obstacles that had broken them up, he'd been thinking about his own future and what he wanted out of it.

That could be summed up in just one word.

Mia.

He wanted everything they had dreamed about. Problem was, he wasn't sure how to make it happen.

Or even if Mia wanted it to happen.

He'd let her down when she'd been at her lowest and hadn't given her what she needed. He'd let his own guilt rule his emotions, and that had resulted in Mia being hurt again when she'd already been struggling to rebuild her life.

Why would she want him back after that?

If he was her, he wasn't sure that he would.

"Julian."

He started and almost stumbled into Mia as she stood, hands planted on her hips, watching him with a mixture of bemusement and mild irritation. Obviously she had said something, and he had missed it because he'd been thinking about them and trying to figure out if he still stood a chance with her.

What he wouldn't give for one more night together. One more kiss, one more exploration of her body—toned to perfection from hours training for her job and spent hiking through the woods searching for lost or injured victims—with his hands and his tongue, one more chance to make love to her and then fall asleep holding her tucked closely against his side.

"Julian," Mia said again. "What is with you tonight?"

"Nothing," he said. If he was going to broach the topic of a possible reconciliation, he certainly wasn't going to do it out here with an unconscious kid in his arms, and a potential kidnapper somewhere close by. "Sorry, what did you say?"

"I was just checking that Devin was still breathing. We don't know what he was given or whether the dosage was appropriate for his size."

That was just one of the many things he loved about Mia. She took her job seriously, cared about every single one of the people she was charged with finding. She worried about them, she made sure to follow up with them after they were safe, and she went to the funerals of anyone who wasn't lucky enough to survive their ordeal.

How had he ever allowed this beautiful, strong, caring, sexy woman to slip through his fingers?

And why hadn't he done something about rectifying it before now?

Rearranging the kid in his arms, he touched his fingertips to Devin's neck and was rewarded by the steady beating of the boy's pulse. "He's okay. How much longer till we get to base?"

"Fifteen minutes. An ambulance and Devin's mother will be there to meet us, and everyone else is already heading back. It's always nice to have a successful search and rescue," she said.

It was.

And while he was glad that they had found Devin alive, all he could think about right now was how easy it would be to lean in and brush his lips across Mia's.

Julian knew he had been stupid to give up on her—on them—now all he had to do was decide if he was going to continue being stupid and let the best thing that had ever happened to him slip away for good, or if he was finally ready to confront his guilt and do whatever it took to get Mia back.

\* \* \* \* \*

9:14 P.M.

Julian was being weird tonight, Mia thought as they approached the base where search and rescue ran all searches from. The building was located about two miles west of the edge of River's End and allowed them plenty of space to run training exercises as well as a nicely centralized location to run searches from.

The fact that her ex was acting weirdly was doing nothing to eliminate her own edginess, although at least she knew the reason she had felt she hadn't been alone was because Julian had been out there too. From the way he had been looking at her as they walked through the forest, she wouldn't have been surprised to find out he had been watching her while she was searching for Devin Deville.

What did that mean?

It had to mean something.

Didn't it?

Or was it just wishful thinking?

Since they had broken up by unspoken agreement, they had both kept their distance from one another, which wasn't easy to do in a small town. Of course, there were times when it was inevitable that their paths would cross, and when they did, it was awkward and stilted and hard to remember that this man had once been someone she had told everything to. There had been no secrets between them, and their relationship had been completely all-encompassing. There wasn't anything she couldn't go to him with, anything she couldn't trust him with, until …

Until it all fell apart.

Mia sighed. There was no point in rehashing old thoughts and feelings, she'd done that enough over the last eighteen months, and she'd come to the conclusion that all it did was open up wounds that were still very precariously healed. She and Julian were over, there was no going back. It didn't make her happy, but it was what it was, and for her own mental health she needed to focus on the future, not the past.

The lights of the base shone through the trees, and a moment later, she stepped out into the clearing and was immediately engulfed in a sea of people. Paramedics took the boy from Julian's arms as Devin's mother wept and grabbed onto her son, clutching his hand in hers as he was laid down on a gurney.

As the boy was taken toward the waiting ambulance, Mia realized Julian was still standing behind her. Uncertain and uncomfortable, unsure what to say or do, a feeling that made her sad since she and Julian had been a couple since high school, Mia looked for a quick and easy out.

"Uh, thanks for being there, it meant we didn't have to wait for the paramedics to come to us and then get back here, so Devin gets to be with his mom quicker and get to the hospital quicker," she said, casting only a brief glance at Julian's face before fixing her gaze on the ground.

When Julian didn't say anything, she dismissed the ache in her chest and turned to head back to the building to unpack her stuff and debrief her team before heading home.

A hand closed around her wrist preventing her from moving, and when she turned back around, she saw Julian watching her with an inscrutable expression on his face. The same odd expression he'd had ever since she'd thrown that rock at him and he'd joined them in the forest.

Tired and unsettled by the night's events, Mia wasn't in the mood for whatever game Julian was playing and moved to tug her arm free.

"Don't." The quiet voice startled her, and her gaze snapped up to Julian's to find his expression had softened and he was looking at her the way he used to back when they were together. The hand encircling her wrist loosened its hold, and his thumb brushed gently across the inside of her wrist, making her shiver.

"What are you doing?" she asked, confused by his behavior tonight.

Julian looked from her down to her arm and seemed to watch his thumb caress her skin before looking back up at her.

Before he could answer, someone yelled out her name, and she looked over her shoulder to see one of her team waving at her.

"We're ready to debrief when you are, Mia," friend and member of her team Eileen Glass called out.

"Be right there," she called back, gently tugging her arm from Julian's grip and immediately missing his touch when she did so. "I have to go debrief my team."

Whatever moment might have been passed, and Julian's gaze had sharpened again. "Since we both touched Devin, our clothes are evidence. I'm going to change before I go to the hospital and put my clothes in an evidence bag. If you wouldn't mind, could you do the same so I can take them with me and pass them on to CSU?"

"Sure," she agreed, wondering why his all-business attitude bothered her. They were over, had been for a while now, and she didn't think that them getting back together was a good idea. The blame for their break up could be laid at both their feet, while she knew Julian wouldn't agree with that assessment it was the truth, and as her therapist reminded her at their monthly sessions, trauma sucked, and the fallout from it always sucked, but the only thing you could do was adjust and keep moving forward.

"Mia … you were great out there, as usual," Julian said, then he left to change and head to the hospital.

Staring after him, Mia had to wonder whether she would ever truly get over him. Just because her ordeal had driven a wedge between them they hadn't been able to overcome, it didn't mean she had stopped loving him. It was just that loving him had morphed into something that caused her pain rather than given her pleasure.

Shaking off the unusual turn of events that had been this rescue, she went inside to the locker room. She always kept a couple of changes of clothes in her locker, partly because this wasn't the only time the cops had commandeered her clothing as part of an active investigation, and partly because hiking through the forest often involved getting wet and dirty. Despite the fact that she was definitely a tomboy who loved the outdoors, she hated to be dirty.

Since this time there was no dirt involved, she bypassed the showers and stripped off her clothes, placing them in one of the evidence bags they kept onsite, and changed into a pair of black sweatpants and a purple long-sleeved t-shirt. Then she popped into one of the toilet stalls, did her business, and washed her hands, then froze as she returned to her locker.

The evidence bag containing her clothes was gone and sitting in its place was a bouquet of her favorite flowers. The pretty little blue flowers had been a favorite of hers since she was in middle school. Even when he was away overseas serving in the marines, Julian would often arrange to have bouquets of bluebells delivered to her, just to let her know that he was thinking about her.

He had to be the one to leave them for her, he must have popped in to get the clothes and left the bouquet. That was so sweet of him, and of course she couldn't not wonder what it meant.

"Mia."

She jolted at the sound and turned to see Eileen standing in the doorway.

"You ready? We're all waiting for you."

"Yes, sorry, of course, I'll be right there," she said, picking up the bouquet to put the flowers in a vase.

"Someone left you flowers?" Eileen asked, looking intrigued

14

now.

"I guess so." She laughed to lighten the knot of tension and longing that had taken up residence in her stomach.

"Lucky girl," Eileen said, then sighed, "I wish someone would leave me flowers."

"It's been a long time since anyone left me any, believe me," she told her friend. Her phone dinged with a message as she followed Eileen out of the locker room and into the foyer.

"I'll take your flowers, so you can check your message, then I'll meet you in the conference room," Eileen offered, holding out a hand to take the bouquet.

Mia handed them over, and while Eileen went toward the kitchen, she stepped over into a corner of the foyer and pulled out her phone. Shock and a small tingling of hope and desire—just a tiny bit, really, minuscule at best—zinged through her when she saw Julian's name on the screen.

The text was short, just three words—Goodnight, sweet dreams—and yet those words wormed their way into her heart. He hadn't wished her sweet dreams since the night before he had packed up his things and announced he was moving out. Although she'd seen it coming, she'd still cried watching him drive away and knowing he wasn't coming back, but now here he was leaving her flowers and telling her goodnight. She had no idea what that meant, wasn't sure it meant anything good, and yet she couldn't wipe the smile off her face as she typed out a quick reply and went to debrief her team.

# OCTOBER 5TH

9:26 A.M.

He might have spent the night in the hospital waiting for Devin Deville to wake up, he might not have had a shower in over twenty-four hours or had his morning cup of coffee, but Julian couldn't stop smiling.

It was all thanks to one little word.

Night.

That was what Mia had replied to his text wishing her a goodnight and sweet dreams, and he liked to think that when she'd heard from him the smile on her face had been the same as the one on his when she'd replied.

It was silly getting so excited over a simple text message, but it felt like the first step toward getting back what he'd lost with Mia.

Julian had sent the text on a whim. As he'd climbed into his car to drive to the hospital, he hadn't been ready to sever the tentative connection he'd been trying to forge with Mia. He knew his odd behavior had thrown her, and he wouldn't have been surprised if he'd scared her off, but when his phone had dinged with a text just moments after he'd sent his, a sense of peace that he hadn't felt in eighteen months had settled over him.

He was doing the right thing.

While Julian knew he should never have let things get to this point, there was also some truth to the saying there was no point crying over spilled milk. All he could do now was work to undo the damage he had caused, which he was sure would involve a lot of apologizing and maybe even some groveling on his part.

"I am now your favorite person," Levi Black, Julian's cousin, announced as he walked down the hospital hallway toward him.

"Yeah? Why?" he asked with a small hint of suspicion. Besides, he was pretty sure that Levi couldn't give him anything that would bump him above Mia on his list of favorite people.

"I have coffee," Levi replied, holding out a Styrofoam cup with steam pouring off it.

"Well, I do like you a little more than I did a moment ago," he told his cousin as he took the cup and greedily took a sip despite the near-boiling temperature of the thick, black liquid.

"See, told you, and that's not even the best part," Levi said with a laugh.

"You got donuts in your pockets?" Julian couldn't see a bright pink paper bag indicating that his cousin had been by the town's cute little bakery on his way to the hospital.

"Nope, no food, but Devin Deville just woke up so you can finally interview him," Levi explained.

Whoever had drugged Devin must have given him a higher dosage than they should have for his size, and the boy had slept through the night. Other than being drugged, Devin didn't have any physical marks on him, and thankfully the exam his mother had finally been persuaded to allow them to perform had shown that he hadn't been sexually assaulted either.

Thank goodness for small mercies.

"Lacey know I'm coming?" he asked as he followed Levi back down the hall toward Devin's room. Devin's mother had been a mess last night, and finding out someone had dosed her son with Rohypnol, the well-known date rape drug, had sent her over the edge. Rohypnol not only incapacitated the victim but also impaired their memory, making it a near-perfect drug for what its abusers intended to use it for.

"She knows you're coming, but she's not happy about it," Levi replied.

"Unfortunately, if she wants to find who kidnapped her son,

18

she doesn't have a choice." Julian wasn't unsympathetic to what Lacey Deville was going through, he didn't have children, but he knew what it was like to have someone you loved snatched away, not knowing if you would ever get them back, and then when you did knowing that they would never be quite the same again.

"Which is why she said I could go and get you when I finished my examination of Devin," Levi said as they walked toward the boy's room.

Julian knew that Lacey wasn't trying to impede their investigation, she was just trying to protect her son, but this interview had to be done, and he hoped that she kept that in mind as he interviewed the child.

"Mo-om, I want Jell-O. Dr. Black said I could have some." Devin was whining when they entered his room.

"Fine," Lacey said on a sigh, but she was smiling at her son, and her eyes were misty.

"How about I go and look for some Jell-O while Deputy Black here asks you a few questions," Levi said. "Lacey, you want to come with me?"

"I'm staying," Lacey replied firmly.

Levi looked to him, and when he gave a small nod, his cousin asked Devin, "Any request on flavor?"

"Lime," Devin replied without hesitation.

Julian studied the boy. He was a little pale, and he looked tired, but other than that he appeared to be none the worse for wear from his ordeal. However, he knew looks could be deceiving. Mia had done the whole I'm fine routine after her ordeal, and it couldn't have been further from the truth.

Taking a seat, he found Devin watching him with a mixture of wariness and curiosity. The wariness no doubt because he knew questions were coming, and Julian also understood the curiosity. When he'd been about Devin's age, he'd been intrigued by anything law-related and had often been jealous of his cousins whose father was the sheriff.

"You know why you're here, Devin?" Julian asked, keeping his tone light.

Devin looked to his mom then back again. "Because I was missing."

"Do you know what that means?"

Devin paused for a moment. "That nobody knew where I was."

"Right, and we want to find out how you got to be missing, so I want you to know that I need you to tell me the truth to every question I ask you. You're not going to get in trouble from me or from your mom for anything that you say." Julian nodded at Lacey, and when Devin turned to look at his mother, she nodded in agreement. "Did you go straight home from school yesterday?"

"I played with my friends in the playground for a bit first, but then I went home, same as I always do," Devin replied.

"Do you remember stopping and talking to anyone on the walk home?"

"No."

"Do you remember anybody watching you, maybe they waved hello, or maybe they were following you in their car, or maybe they showed you something, like a puppy?" It was surprising how often the, come and see my puppy ruse worked; people were suckers for a puppy.

Devin shook his head slowly. "No, I don't remember anyone. I just remember walking home, and then I was waking up here, and my mom was crying."

Although he was disappointed by the boy's answers he wasn't surprised. They knew the fact he had been given Rohypnol meant he would likely have zero memories of the abduction. "Is there anyone who might make you go missing, Devin, someone who makes you feel uncomfortable or even scared?"

"No," Devin said confidently, but Julian caught a look on Lacey's face that said she thought otherwise.

Levi came breezing into the room, Jell-O cup in hand and

Julian took advantage of that. "Lacey, while Dr. Black gives Devin his treat could I speak with you briefly in the hall?"

Lacey looked conflicted, but Devin was already distracted by his snack so she kissed his cheek and then followed Julian out into the hall.

"You think you know who took your son?" he asked without preamble. He had tried to talk to Lacey last night, but she had been hysterical, and he hadn't been able to get anything useful out of her.

"I don't want to think this, I really don't. Believing that he could do this makes me question every decision I ever made in my life," she said, tears brimming in her eyes.

"But?" he prompted.

"My husband—well, *ex*-husband now—and I got divorced about two months ago, he wasn't happy when I was given full physical custody, and he was only allowed visitation every second weekend. We have joint legal custody, but he wanted Devin to spend more time with him. I got custody because I work from home and it's easier for me to be able to care for Devin's needs, but Vince was angry about it. He said he could change his whole schedule to be there for Devin, he went back to court just a week or two ago to try to change the custody agreement. I would never try to keep Devin from his father. Despite our problems and inability to make our marriage work, I thought Vince was a good dad. It was just practicalities that made it easier for me to be the primary caregiver at this point in our lives. Do you think he could have taken Devin? I mean, whoever it was didn't hurt him, so it could have been Vince. Maybe he was going to abduct Devin, take him far away, but he got interrupted by the search teams before he could get away. Or maybe he was going to take Devin, but then he backed out, realized he couldn't deprive our son of his mother." Lacey stared at him with imploring eyes, begging him to give her the answers she needed.

But he couldn't.

Because he didn't have any yet.

However, he did know where to go to get some.

Interviewing Vince Deville just became the day's top priority.

\* \* \* \* \*

10:34 A.M.

"Tell me there's chocolate," Mia said as her friend Meadow Black opened the door to the small cabin in the forest, she shared with her husband and town sheriff Abe, and four-month-old daughter Dawn.

"Well there is," Meadow said as she ushered Mia inside, "but Maggie is currently going through a chocolate makes her nauseous phase."

Mia winced. This was another in a long line of foods that Maggie hadn't been able to stand to be in the same room as since she'd gotten pregnant. She had no idea how Theo managed to live in the same house with her and not lose weight since what Maggie could and couldn't eat changed almost with each passing day.

"Does that mean chocolate is a no-go today?" she asked in a voice that was close to a whine. She had hardly slept last night thanks to a certain sexy deputy who had left her all hot and bothered and unable to sleep.

"No way, if my girl needs chocolate she gets chocolate," Maggie said with a grin as they walked into the living room where her friends were waiting for their monthly catch-up lunch.

"I don't want you to feel sick," Mia said, dropping down onto one end of the sofa.

"Rough day?" Renee asked.

She and Renee had always been close, almost like sisters, and she'd been so upset when everything had gone down with Renee and Will. She was so glad they had managed to work through it all and got back together.

"Yeah, kind of," she said, reaching for a cupcake.

"Then you're in good company." Sydney Clark huffed as she came in from the kitchen with a tray filled with cups of coffee.

"Uh-oh," Mia said as she took a mug of steaming coffee and blew on it. "What did Levi do?"

Sydney huffed before flicking her brown locks over her shoulder and taking a seat on the other sofa. Sydney had moved to River's End a few months earlier and immediately caught the eye of resident sexy doctor Levi Black.

"He still hasn't proposed?" Meadow asked as she checked the baby monitor on the table.

"No, and I know we've only known each other for four months, but we both know we're committed to each other, and I thought he would have done it by now," Sydney said.

"He's probably planning something really special," Poppy suggested. She and her parents had moved to River's End when she was twelve, but she'd lost her parents in a car accident earlier in the year, and while off in California laying them to rest had met the love of her life. "At least that's what I tell myself when I start getting worried that Beau hasn't proposed yet."

"Not everyone proposes at warp speed like our guys," Renee said, indicating herself, Meadow, and Maggie. Will had proposed to Renee within days of them reconnecting, but given that they'd been a couple all of their adult lives and he had been planning on proposing before a bad decision led to the end of their relationship, it made sense.

"If I hadn't been pregnant and we didn't want to be married before the baby came, then I don't think Abe would have proposed and married me within four months of dating," Meadow said.

"And even though Theo and I had been friends all our lives, if I hadn't wound up pregnant a month after we got together I don't think he would have proposed so soon," Maggie added. She and Theo were getting married a couple of days before Christmas.

"I know, I just get so insecure sometimes. I really thought Levi would have proposed before now." Sydney dropped her head into her hands and rubbed her temples. "Men."

"Yeah, men," Renee agreed.

"What did Will do?" Poppy asked.

"He's just always so protective, worrying about everything. We had a fight this morning when I forgot to set the alarm while he went to buy bread because we'd run out and I need to start my day with toast," Renee explained.

"Given what happened to you just a couple of months ago I can't say I blame him for being paranoid," Maggie said.

Renee sighed but then gave a small nod. "Yeah, I guess."

"Theo still worries about me," Maggie admitted. "It doesn't help that I still have nightmares."

"I do too," Renee said.

"Me three," Poppy said.

"Ditto," Meadow said and shuddered, her fingers absently tracing a scar on her arm.

"Me too," Sydney said. "They get worse any time I have to go to another appointment for my burns. I hate it. I'm a cop, I'm not supposed to still be freaked out about that."

"It doesn't work that way," Renee reminded her. "Trauma sticks with you, time only dulls it, it doesn't take it away."

Wasn't that the truth.

It had been two years since her own brush with trauma, and she still had the occasional nightmare. While she didn't think about it every day anymore, she still had triggers, and every now and then, something would make all of those feelings and fears come rushing back.

She hated those moments.

When they hit, she could no longer delude herself into believing she was over it.

"You know what?" Renee asked.

"What?" Poppy asked.

"I kind of like when Will worries. I mean, yeah it makes me so mad sometimes, but it's nice to have him there. I don't know how I would have gotten through this without him, and if that means I have to put up with a little over-protectiveness, I'll take it," Renee said, and she smiled as she obviously thought about Will and how much they loved each other.

Mia missed that.

Missed having someone to hold her when she had a nightmare, missed having someone to bother her about being safe, missed having someone worry about her, missed having someone who cared where she was and what she was doing.

She missed Julian.

It was stupid, they'd had their chance, and they'd blown it, and yet after yesterday she couldn't stop thinking about him. About them. She couldn't seem to get him out of her mind.

But right now, she was feeling a little jealous of her friends and embarrassed, she pushed to her feet and hurried out of the room, heading upstairs to the bathroom.

Since she didn't really have to go, she stared at herself in the mirror. She was thirty, divorced—well separated since she had never filed the divorce papers—and childless. This wasn't how she had pictured her life turning out when Julian had proposed to her on the night of their high school graduation.

It was Meadow and Abe's, his and hers toothbrushes in the little flower holder that finally cracked her composure.

Tears brimmed in her eyes and she brushed them away, annoyed. She didn't want to cry. Didn't really even have anything to cry about. So she and Julian hadn't worked out, lots of high school sweethearts didn't.

Knowing that if she didn't head back downstairs one of her friends would come looking for her to check she was okay, Mia ran some cold water and splashed it on her face. She didn't begrudge her friends their happiness. They had all gone through a lot to get where they were, she just hoped that her happy ending was around the corner.

On the stairs, she met Renee. "Everything okay?" her friend asked.

Mia opened her mouth, intending to lie. It would be so easy to say she was a little on edge after the Devin case the night before. They probably wouldn't believe her, but they wouldn't push her, knowing she would talk when she was ready. But instead of a lie the truth came out.

"Julian left me flowers yesterday after we found Devin Deville in the forest and he was taken to the hospital," she blurted out.

"Wow." Renee's dark eyes grew wide and then she grinned. "That is so awesome."

"Awesome?" she echoed. That wasn't quite how Mia would describe it. If she had to pick one word it would be confusing. "He also texted me goodnight."

"Ooh," Renee squealed like they were back in high school again. "We have to talk about this with the others."

Mia followed Renee back down to the living room. Poppy, Sydney, Maggie, and Meadow all looked up when she came in, and she knew that she'd made the right choice in deciding to talk to her friends. That was the point of having friends, they were a sounding board when you needed to make a potentially life-altering decision, or support you when someone hurt you.

"Julian left flowers for Mia," Renee exclaimed.

Everyone's faces lit up. "We need details," Meadow said.

"All of them," Poppy added.

"Absolutely. Don't leave anything out," Sydney agreed as she opened up a block of chocolate and began to pass some to everyone. "Sorry, Mags."

"Don't be. I'll breathe through my mouth and try not to smell it," Maggie said. "Mia, start at the beginning."

So she did. She started at the beginning, prepared to tell her friends everything and hoped they could help her figure this out.

* * * * *

1:41 P.M.

Julian checked the time on his phone. Nine minutes since he'd last looked, he was starting to think that Vince Deville had decided to go on the run. If the man was behind his son's abduction, then he might have realized that they were onto him.

Right now, Vince kidnapping Devin was the scenario that made the most sense. Devin hadn't been harmed, and he'd been left where someone would find him. That would most likely only have been done by someone who cared about him. The custody case was the perfect stressor to have set Vince off, which meant that he had the motive to do this, as well as the means since yesterday was Vince's day off.

With a sigh, he twisted in the driver's seat of his car to look up and down the street, but there was no sign of Vince's car. His mind wandered back to the same topic that had occupied it almost continuously for the last twenty-four hours.

Mia.

This morning he had thought about checking in, see how she had done last night. Mia didn't have any idea yet that they thought it was a parental abduction so she was no doubt worrying about what Devin had endured, but in the end, he hadn't gone through with it. He'd taken the first step in reaching out, trying to forge a new tentative bond, now it was her turn.

He knew that sounded silly, childish even, but he needed to know that this was what she wanted.

Before he could cave and pull his phone back out and shoot off a text to Mia, he saw Vince's car approaching.

Finally.

Now they could get some answers.

As Vince pulled into the driveway of his small single-story ranch house, Julian climbed out of his car and walked across the lawn to meet him on the small porch.

"Hey, Vince," he announced himself. One of the things you had to get used to as a small-town deputy was questioning people that you knew. Vince was a couple of years younger than him, but they'd gone to school together, played together in the forest as kids, and while Julian didn't exactly consider the other man a friend they were more than just acquaintances.

"Julian." Vince nodded but then his gaze narrowed. "From the look on your face, I'm going to say this isn't a social call."

"Where were you last night, Vince?" he asked, ignoring the comment.

Vince shrugged. "I was out of town yesterday, I needed some space to clear my head so I went for a drive, slept over in a motel, then drove back today. What's going on?" Vince's eyes grew wide and he gasped. "Is it Devin? Did something happen to my son?"

"Why don't we go inside, sit down, talk," he suggested.

"No," Vince said, his spine going ramrod straight. "Tell me. Is Devin hurt? Dead?"

"Vince, let's go inside," he said firmly in a voice that brokered no argument. He wasn't having this conversation standing in Vince's front yard.

For a moment, it looked like Vince was going to argue and Julian had to remember that this was a dangerous man—or at least a desperate man which made him dangerous—who might be violent, even if it was out of a sense of self-preservation. But then Vince's shoulders slumped, and he unlocked the door and led him into a cramped living room.

The house was a lot smaller than the one Vince used to share with his wife and son. In the divorce settlement, Lacey had been given the house because she had owned it before the marriage and Vince hadn't contested the decision, but this was definitely a downgrade. Three doors led off the living room. He assumed two went to bedrooms—one Vince's and the other for Devin when he visited—and the other to a bathroom. The kitchen was nothing more than a kitchenette, then there was a dining table, a sofa, and a large screen TV on an entertainment stand with a bunch of electronics around it. It was clear where most of Vince's money went, gadgets for his son.

"Okay, we're inside, and I'm sitting down. Now tell me if my son is okay," Vince demanded.

Julian joined him on the other end of the sofa. "Devin is alive, but he's in the hospital."

"The hospital?" Vince shouted, darting to his feet. "What happened? Was he in an accident? Did someone hurt him?"

At the moment, Julian couldn't tell if Vince was being sincere or just playing dumb. "Devin was grabbed on his way home from school." Julian held up a hand to stop Vince when he would have blurted out a mass of questions. "Search and rescue was called in immediately. The search was focused around where Devin's school bag was found. We found him within a few hours, he was unconscious, someone had drugged him. He spent the night in the hospital so he could be monitored as the drugs worked their way out of his system."

"So he's okay?" Vince asked, desperation on his face.

"He's okay. Whoever took him didn't do anything other than take him and drug him." Julian stopped talking and waited Vince out, hoping to get a read on him based on his reaction and how quickly he admitted that he was the number one suspect.

All the color drained from Vince's face. "You think I kidnapped my own son? Why would I do that?"

"You're in the middle of a custody case," he reminded the other man. "Lacey said that you were unhappy with the fact that while you share legal custody, she has sole physical custody. She said you had petitioned the court to change the arrangement and had changed your work schedule so you could be around for Devin more. Did you get afraid that you would lose, Vince? Were you afraid you would be phased out of your son's life? Did you decide to take matters into your own hands? Did you take him,

Vince? Did you drug him and intend to run off with him? Did you get scared and back out and leave him in the woods, or did you get interrupted when you saw Mia walking around too close and thought if you didn't leave him you'd get caught?"

Vince glared at him. "I wouldn't hurt my son like that."

"Desperate times and all that."

"I wasn't desperate," Vince declared.

"No?"

"No. I would have gotten joint custody, there was no reason I wouldn't. They should have given us joint custody in the beginning," Vince fumed. "Do you know how much I have to pay in child support to Lacey? I can barely afford this place by the time it gets taken out of my paycheck. I want to be able to give my son a good life, I want to be able to take him on vacations and buy him the things he wants. Lacey claimed that since she worked from home, she could give our son something I couldn't but that wasn't fair. I deserved joint custody, and Devin wanted to spend more time with me. That's why I filed."

All Julian heard was desperation, it dripped from every word he said, seeped from every pore in his body. He felt like he was missing out on his child's life, he felt like he had been dealt an unfair hand, he seemed like he was teetering on the edge, and Julian could buy that he had decided to take matters into his own hands.

"You don't believe me," Vince said.

"Devin wasn't hurt, he was given Rohypnol, that would have made him easier to deal with, made sure he wouldn't fight back, and it would have wiped his memories which means when you got him wherever it was you planned on taking him he wouldn't remember that you kidnapped him."

"I didn't kidnap my son," Vince growled. "I would never do anything to hurt my son. Devin loves his mother, I would never deprive him of that, it's why I only asked for joint custody and not full. I didn't want to cut her out, I just wanted us to be equal parents. I rearranged my whole work schedule so I could be around for Devin when he got home from school each day. Without having to pay exorbitant child support I could buy us a bigger place. Devin could have more room, more things, we would have been so happy. It all would have worked out. It would have."

Only there was no way that Vince could know that for sure.

He had seen before just what a desperate parent who felt like they were backed up against a wall would do, and it wasn't always pretty.

Right now, given what Vince had just told him he still considered Devin's father to be the number one suspect in his abduction. If Vince wasn't going to admit to anything, they needed to find some sort of physical evidence to get a conviction.

\* \* \* \* \*

4:16 P.M.

As she pulled into her driveway, Mia could honestly say she was more confused than ever about the whole Julian situation now than she had been when she arrived at Meadow's house for lunch.

Her friends had been great, letting her rehash everything that had led up to their break up, everything she had felt and rebuilt over the last eighteen months, and what had happened last night, how odd Julian had been acting, and then the flowers and the text. They had offered opinions, let her bounce ideas off them, but what they couldn't do was help her decide what to do next.

Because ultimately, only she could make that decision.

Resting her head back against the seat, she closed her eyes and tried to decide on a course of action. The problem was, she didn't know what Julian wanted. Yes, he had reached out, albeit tentatively, but all he had really done was leave her some flowers and wished her a goodnight. It could just be him wanting to make sure she was okay after finding Devin's body, it could be him wanting the two of them to be friends, or it could be him wanting to get back together.

Although as Poppy had pointed out, he had to have had the flowers with him when he came to join the search. There was a florist in town, which would have been closed by the time they found Devin, and even if it was open, there wasn't any time for him to have driven into town, bought flowers, and got back all in the time it took her to change and go to the bathroom.

So logic dictated he'd brought them with him. Julian would have known she'd be there. As the head of the search and rescue unit, she was present for every single search, so he must have been thinking about her before he saw her that night. Was that why he was being weird? Because he wanted to talk to her about them?

She groaned and shoved open the door, getting out of the car and dragging in a couple of mouthfuls of chilly fall air. With the beginning of fall came the start of sweater season, pumpkin carving, open fireplaces, and Halloween at the end of the month.

Of course she couldn't think of Halloween and not recall all the Black family Halloween parties she had attended over the years. Every year for as long as she could remember, Julian's aunt and uncle had held a Halloween party. As kids, they'd dress up, play games, run through the haunted maze, and eat way more junk than they should have both before and after trick-or-treating. The older they'd gotten, the more the party had changed until, as adults, they had mostly just dressed up and hung out and had dinner.

She'd missed that party last year.

That was the problem with breaking up with a long-term partner. You didn't just lose them but their family too.

Tired of rerunning the same thoughts through her head over and over again, Mia pushed them away and walked through her small front yard. It wasn't much, just grass which she paid someone to mow every two weeks, and two large trees, one on either side of the path that led from the sidewalk to the porch. Right now, the trees were turning every amazing color that made fall her favorite season, and she took a moment to stand in the yard and soak in the beauty of this time of year.

This was why she loved small-town life, the peace and tranquility, the quaint little stores, the way everybody knew everybody. She loved that the blocks of land were all larger with yards for kids to play in and that you didn't have to drive more than about ten minutes in any direction to be back out in the forest. Mia couldn't imagine living anywhere else.

She couldn't stand out there all evening. She had some paperwork to attend to and had to decide whether she would do it here at home or down at the base. It was probably better to go down there, she'd be able to concentrate better, but she didn't feel like getting back in her car again once she collected what she needed to so she decided she'd stay here, work for a while, eat a light dinner—she was still full after lunch—then go for a run before heading to bed.

Pleased that she had a plan to keep her mind occupied so she didn't spend any more time obsessing over Julian, she headed to the front door.

As soon as she walked up the three steps to the porch she saw them.

A large bouquet of flowers sat on her doorstep.

These ones were all different types of flowers, but each and every one of them was pink. Julian knew that pink was her favorite color, in fact it had been a sticking point for them over the years. He'd hated sleeping on pink sheets in a bedroom with pink paint on the walls and pink carpet.

Unable to stop a smile from curving her lips up, Mia scooped up the bouquet, holding it close to her nose as she breathed in the sweet, flowery fragrance. A second bouquet of flowers in as many days, that had to mean that Julian was interested in seeing if maybe enough time had passed that they could find a way to work through the issues that had torn them apart. She really couldn't think of any other explanation which meant she had a lot of soul searching to do.

Did she want to get back with Julian?

Could they work through their issues?

So much had been said and done and she wasn't sure it was possible to go back.

Yet, at the same time, she wasn't sure it was impossible.

Hope was a precious thing, and sometimes it needed a lot of nurturing and some tender love and care. As she unlocked the door, let herself in, and reset the alarm behind her, she knew that she wasn't going to get a lot of work done tonight.

Instead of heading to her home office, she made her way through to the kitchen, poured herself a glass of apple juice, then sunk into the window seat as she dialed her dad's number.

Her mom had died when Mia was two, much too young to remember her, but her dad had done such a great job of being both her father and her mother, and she'd never really felt like she was missing out growing up. Julian had also lost his mother young, and it had been something they'd been able to bond over. They had also both been taken under the wing of Julian's aunt Tatiana who had stepped up and been a mother figure for both of them when they needed it.

Mia was definitely a daddy's girl, and when she felt like she wasn't in control she reached out to him.

"Hey, princess." Her dad's voice came down the line, and she felt herself settle.

"Hey, daddy, how are you feeling today?" Her father had been diagnosed with stage four pancreatic cancer almost four months ago, and while she had been begging him to come and move in with her, her dad was stubborn and hadn't been ready to give up his independence.

"I'm fine, baby girl," he said, brushing off her concerns like he always did. Losing his wife and raising a daughter on his own had been hard for him but he had never complained. He found a way to balance work and being a single father and always had given her everything she needed. "To what do I owe the pleasure of a phone call from my favorite girl?"

Mia sighed but smiled. "I'm your only girl, dad," she reminded him. Her father had never remarried, never even dated, after losing his wife, Mia's mom was his soul mate, his other half, and he hadn't even wanted to look for love again. Kind of like her. While she hadn't lost Julian to death she had lost him, and hadn't even been able to look at another man. Julian was her soul mate.

"Still my favorite," her father said on a laugh, but she could hear the pain in his voice. He was hurting, and his diagnosis was terminal. She *was* going to lose him, and when she did, she would be all alone in the world, she and Julian were still married but on paper only.

"What's bothering you, princess?"

"Julian's been leaving me flowers," she blurted out. Her dad had been upset when she and Julian broke up and had hoped they would find a way to work things out, so she knew he would be thrilled with this development.

True to form, she could practically hear his grin down the line. "Well, well, well, about time that boy realized what he lost when he left you."

"It was both our fault things ended up the way they did," Mia reminded him.

"But *you're* my baby girl," her dad said. "I'm glad, princess, you two love each other so much, and I would hate to see that man take anything else from you."

The man her father was referring to was a stalker who had harassed her relentlessly for almost a year before she had been forced to kill him in a desperate fight for survival.

She didn't want to think about him right now.

"It's complicated though, dad," she said.

"Do you still love him?"

"You know I do."

"Then it's not complicated."

Her father made it sound so simple, but it wasn't. Sometimes love wasn't enough to undo shattered trust.

"You're wrong, baby girl," her dad said. "Love is enough. There wasn't anything that your mom could have done that would make me stop loving her. I would have done anything to keep her in my life, anything."

"But that's just it, Dad, I did love Julian, and he didn't stay, he left. I'm not saying that I wasn't partly to blame for that, but he's the one who left. When I needed him he wasn't there. And now, I don't know how to trust him again. I want to, I want everything to go back to the way things were before, but I don't know if we can, and that makes me scared to try."

"Fear is a part of life, princess, but you have to decide whether you're going to give in to it or work through it."

Problem was she wasn't sure if she was strong enough to work through it.

\* \* \* \* \*

7:02 P.M.

"H-hmm," Julian cleared his throat to get his brother and his fiancée's attention.

"Sorry, man," Will said, turning and giving him a sheepish smile.

"Forgot I was here, huh?" Julian teased. He and Will had left the station at the same time, and Julian had followed him back here to have dinner with his brother and Renee, but as soon as the two saw each other they'd started kissing, leaving him on the doorstep, waiting to get in out of the chilly evening.

"Sorry, Julian," Renee said, "but in my defense I did make your favorite dinner."

"Ribs?" His mouth was watering at the thought, he'd been so busy today he'd skipped lunched, and the only thing he'd eaten was the donuts Levi had given him at the hospital this morning.

"Yep, and as a bonus I'm full from lunch with the girls so there'll probably be plenty of leftovers so you can take some home with you."

"Only if I don't eat them all," Will said with a grin.

"You wouldn't dare," he mock growled at his older brother, but his mind was lingering on the fact that Renee had no doubt seen Mia today. Had they talked about him? He knew women talked when they were together, and since he had made a tentative attempt to reach out to her yesterday he was sure that she had to be thinking about him as much as he was thinking about her.

"I might, but if I did, Renee would probably never make me ribs again," Will said as they all headed into the kitchen.

"That's true," Renee agreed cheerfully as she started dishing up plates for all of them.

"What do you want to drink?" Will asked as he went to the fridge.

"Whatever you're having," he replied as he watched the two of them bustle around the kitchen. He missed those simple domestic moments like this, preparing for dinner, nothing exciting, just cooking, hanging out, being together. While he wasn't really much of a cook, he'd loved making dinner with Mia just because they got to be together without any distractions and intrusions.

In between working this case Julian had been consumed with thoughts of Mia and indecisions about what his next move should be. He wanted to reach out again, but he just wasn't sure if he should. If this wasn't what Mia wanted, then he didn't want to get his hopes up.

Any more than he already had anyway.

Although he hadn't thought much about getting back with Mia

until Will and Renee had reconnected a couple of months ago, he'd missed her every day since he'd packed his bags and left. Missing her was like missing a part of himself. They'd been together practically all their lives, and he'd never been with another woman. They'd been a couple since he asked her to the Christmas dance in eighth grade. Sure they'd had plenty of ups and downs in their teenage years, but by the time they were adults they had settled into a groove where everything ran smoothly. They'd married after he completed boot camp, and they'd handled his deployment without issues. He'd thought that if they could get through that, they could get through anything.

How wrong he had been.

"Mia kept doing that today too."

Julian blinked and realized that Renee had said something. "Sorry, I was just thinking."

"I know, that's what I said. Mia kept zoning out today too."

He didn't know what to say to that, mostly because he didn't know what Mia had already told Renee. "She was a little upset about the Deville search last night," he said vaguely.

"Understandable, but I'm pretty sure that wasn't what kept distracting her," Renee said as she set the plates on the table and they all sat down.

"You and Mia getting back together?" Will asked.

Julian opened his mouth to say no but found he couldn't make the word come out because, yeah, he wanted to get back with her. He loved her, didn't want to live his life without her, he wanted the family they had always talked about, problem was he just didn't know if it could happen.

Had too much damage already been done?

He had walked away when she was dealing with a horrific ordeal, and he wasn't sure how to forgive himself for that. It wasn't the first time he hadn't been there when someone he loved needed him, and his failures with Mia had only compounded his already existing feelings of failure.

"Well, since you jumped into an answer to that question I'm going to guess that things between you two aren't going the way you hoped," Will said.

"It's not that, it's just ..." he trailed off as he tried to figure out how to put into words what he was feeling. If anyone would understand his situation with Mia it was definitely Will and Renee, and he trusted both of them, valued their input. "I have been thinking about her a lot since you two got back together, and I did kind of reach out to her last night, but I don't know if it's too late."

"You were the main topic of conversation at lunch today," Renee said.

"And?" he prompted when she didn't say more.

"And Mia is confused too. I think you two need to sit down and talk, figure out what you both want and how to make it happen," Renee said.

Well, that was a uselessly vague answer.

"So does Mia want to get back together or not?" he asked.

"She wants to know what you want," Renee replied.

Will choked on a laugh. "You two were always the worst at making decisions. I remember going supermarket shopping with you guys. Julian, do we want vanilla ice cream or chocolate ice cream? Whatever you want, babe. I don't mind, you can choose. No, you choose, I'm happy with either. So am I so you pick. Ugh," Will groaned, "it was a nightmare."

His brother wasn't wrong, he and Mia had been bad at making decisions, but this was a lot bigger than just choosing a flavor of ice cream. "We do need to talk," he agreed. "But right now, I don't know what to say to her. I want her back, but I don't know if I deserve another chance."

"Why wouldn't you?" Will asked.

"Do you really have to ask that? I let her down. She was stalked for a year, abducted, raped, and forced to kill her tormentor, and what did I do? I left."

"That's putting a bad spin on things," Will said with a frown. "That's not quite the way I remember things going."

"I left, didn't I?"

"Yeah, okay, you left, but you didn't just pack up and leave right away. Trauma changes things, it makes you doubt everything, it takes your life and tosses it into your own personal tornado and leaves you to pick up the pieces," Will said.

"I don't think Mia is angry with you," Renee said. "And she said it was both of your fault that things fell apart."

That sounded just like something Mia would say, even if it couldn't be more wrong. "She was the one who went through hell, I should have stayed." Leaving had been the hardest thing he had ever done, but at the time it had seemed like the only option he had.

"You both suffered when Mia was being stalked," Will said. "And it's not a competition. Things were messed up for both of you back then. What you have to focus on is now. What do you want? Right now, you're kind of wishy-washy because you're trying to figure out what's going on in Mia's head instead of focusing on what's going on inside your own."

His brother wasn't wrong.

He had been trying to decide what to do next based on what he thought Mia wanted.

"When Renee came back to town I knew from the second that I saw her again that I wanted her back. I was prepared to do whatever it took because I didn't want to spend another day without her. I eventually wore her down." Will grinned and slung an arm around Renee's shoulders, kissing her cheek.

Renee smiled back at her fiancé and the love between them was clear. Will had also walked away from Renee at a low point in her life, albeit to do something he thought was important, but she'd been able to forgive him, and they'd been able to rebuild their love and trust. Maybe that meant things weren't completely hopeless for him and Mia.

"One thing I had to work on was forgiving myself for letting down the woman I loved," Will added.

"It wasn't easy, Julian, but Will and I were able to get past what happened, and you and Mia can too if it's what you both want," Renee said. "But Will is right, you do have to forgive yourself. Mia already has, so that's not the issue standing between the two of you getting back together."

No, that issue was him.

Him and the guilt he had carried around since childhood.

He hadn't been able to stop his mother's death.

He hadn't been able to prevent Mia from nearly losing her life.

And he couldn't forgive himself for either one.

# OCTOBER 6TH

8:35 A.M.

"Mia, we got another one."

She looked up from her desk to see her friend Eileen standing in the office doorway. It had been a long night with little sleep on the back of the previous night's lack of sleep, and her mind was a little fuzzy this morning. "Another what?"

"Another kid missing," Eileen explained.

That had her straightening in her seat. That didn't make any sense. She'd spoken with the Sheriff and found out that Devin's abduction was thought to have been committed by his father because Vince felt like he was being shoved out of his son's life. Abe had said they thought that either her presence had made Vince panic and leave Devin, or he had left the boy where he knew he would be found because he'd realized he couldn't go through with the kidnapping.

If that was the case, how could there be another missing child?

"Another kid missing?" she asked, sure her sleep-deprived brain must be mishearing things.

"Eight-year-old Parker Barrett," Eileen said. "Was reported missing when he didn't meet up with his best friend and the boy's mother. Apparently, when his mom has to leave for work he walks around the block and walks to school with his friend's family. When Parker didn't show up like he always did, the friend's mom called Parker's mom, and she said he left on time like he always did."

This was crazy.

Two missing little boys in three days.

"And why do we think he's missing out here?" Mia asked.

"His schoolbag was found close to where Devin's was," Eileen replied.

What did that mean?

Was Devin's abduction not committed by his father?

Were they looking at some sort of serial abductor?

And what was this person going to do to the children?

Devin hadn't been physically harmed, but he was the first missing child, and that could easily be explained by the fact that the kidnapper had been scared, nervous, unable to do whatever he had planned. But the more children that went missing, the more confidence he would gain, and then they would have injured—or dead—boys on their hands.

Shoving her chair back, her paperwork already forgotten, Mia fell easily into her role as leader of the team, putting in phone calls and planning out a search grid, the same one they had used the other night when they searched for Devin Deville.

In just thirty minutes her team had assembled, been briefed, and they were all heading off into the forest, praying that they were going to get the same result as last time.

Mia had only just lost sight of the base when she felt it, that eerie sensation of being watched.

She shivered despite the mild morning and looked around, not noticing anything out of the ordinary.

The sense of déjà vu had her shuddering again, and she had to force herself to pull it together.

It was just the lingering uncomfortable feeling from the other night that had her on edge. That night, assuming his father committed Devin's abduction, she might actually have been being watched. She'd scared Vince off or he'd seen her and knew it was safe to leave Devin knowing he would soon be found, but today there was nobody out there, nobody watching her, she was alone, and she had to get a handle on this creepy feeling before it started to mess with her ability to do her job.

Masking any apprehension on her face—just in case she really was being watched—she started walking, calling Parker's name as she went. There was no way to know if Parker's abduction was related to Devin's. His father could have still taken Devin, but whoever took Parker could be someone completely different.

Someone with more nefarious purposes.

While she didn't agree with Vince kidnapping his own son, she could understand his frustrations at feeling like he was being pushed to the sidelines in his child's life. It didn't make snatching Devin okay. His son would never be the same person again thanks to the ordeal, but it made sense, and Vince wouldn't have physically harmed the boy, but Parker might not be so lucky.

Was he out there somewhere?

Had he already been hurt?

Was he still alive?

Had his abductor already fled the town and taken the boy somewhere where he would never be found?

With renewed determination, Mia kept walking. If Parker was out here, she and her team would find him and ensure that he got the medical assistance he needed.

Over her years in search and rescue, she had walked through these woods so many times. She'd even searched for people she knew and cared about. She'd found people who hadn't survived, and she'd found people with horrific injuries. She'd pulled people out of the river and out from under piles of snow. She had searched for missing children who had wandered away from a campsite, men out fishing for the weekend, and whole families who had veered off paths and gotten lost. Despite all of that, this was the tensest she had ever been on a search.

This was different.

She wasn't looking for someone who was lost or hurt, she was looking for someone who had been taken against their will.

Besides parent abductions, adults only took kids for one

reason, and that one reason had dread pooling in her stomach. Finding a child who had just been assaulted was not something that she wanted to do, and she found herself wishing that Julian was here with her.

Julian would know what to do, he was always so calm and controlled in any situation. He was a cop, he'd dealt with victims before, and he would know what to do and what to say to Parker when they found him.

He would also know what to do and say to her to help her calm down.

She was never like this when she was working. She was good at her job, knew how to track, wasn't afraid of the elements, she knew how to take care of herself out here no matter how remote things got, and she was trained well enough in first aid that she could deal with most situations. The fact that she was suddenly fighting off panic attacks while out in the forest that was like a second home to her worried her. And she couldn't even blame Julian because she'd been feeling this way the other day before she and Julian had their … moment.

Despite the feeling of not being alone out here that wouldn't budge, Mia continued walking, scanning the area as she went, and calling out Parker's name.

She'd been walking for close to forty-five minutes when she spotted him.

Parker Barrett was lying on the ground, close to the trunk of a large tree. He wasn't moving, and dread pooled in her stomach.

"Parker?" she called out as she checked the area for any threats before rushing to the little boy's side. He didn't answer, and when she dropped to her knees, she found his eyes closed and his hands folded and resting on his stomach. She could see them rising with each breath he took, but still she touched her fingertips to his neck to check for a pulse.

Relief rushed through her, Parker was alive, and she couldn't see any blood or other notable injuries, and he was fully dressed.

He looked just like Devin had and she would bet anything that Parker had been drugged and left out here by the same person who had taken Devin. While she had no idea what that meant and was glad it wasn't her job to figure it out, she slipped comfortably into her role. Covering the boy with a blanket, she radioed in that she had found Parker and given her location so that a team could come in and carry the child out.

Then she settled down onto the ground to wait.

Now that she didn't have anything to do but wait for a team to arrive, her nerves were back on edge. Someone was watching her, she would swear to it if she had to, but even though she was constantly scanning their surroundings, she couldn't see them.

Mia knew she had to be imagining it, there was no logical or rational reason for whoever had abducted Parker to still be nearby or to be watching her, yet she couldn't stop the feeling. What was wrong with her? She hadn't felt this out of control since she had been stalked two years ago.

There was no way she was going back to that place.

The place where she lived in constant fear and uncertainty. It was hell there, knowing there was no way to stop what was happening because you didn't know who was doing it to you. There wasn't much the cops could do about flowers and gifts being left at her house, her job, and in her car if she went out someplace. They couldn't stop the phone calls, notes, or emails, and changing her number didn't do any good.

But she wasn't in that place anymore.

Her stalker was dead, she knew because she was the one who had pulled the trigger.

No one was watching her.

Didn't matter how many times she told herself that, the feeling didn't dissipate, and she just sat there waiting and wishing that Julian was here to wrap an arm around her and tell her she was safe with him.

When he said it she believed it, but he wasn't here, and she was alone with an unconscious child with nothing to do but wait.

* * * * *

10:10 A.M.

Julian jumped out of his car the second he turned the engine off, wrangled with his seatbelt, which seemed to have chosen this particular moment to become uncooperative, then ran the short distance to where a couple of the men from Mia's search and rescue team stood.

"News?" he asked without preamble.

"Mia found him," Rex Stevens replied.

"And?" A million scenarios were running through his head as he tried to make sense of this latest development in his case. If it was a development in his case. His gut screamed there had to be a connection because he didn't believe in coincidence, and two young boys going missing within days of each other meant they had to be related, but he liked Devin's father Vince for his abduction and why would Vince abduct another boy?

"Found same way as Devin Deville. Lying unconscious, most likely drugged, but otherwise unharmed," Lyle Ronald explained. Lyle was already planning a huge seventy-fifth birthday bash for himself in January and had been on the search and rescue team since it was first established coming on fifty years ago, with no signs of slowing down. When Mia had first been asked to take over as leader of the team she had been worried that Lyle would object, she was young, and a woman, and Lyle had already been passed over once before, but the man had happily welcomed her to the job and supported her one hundred percent.

Was Devin's abduction not related to the custody case?

Was Parker Barrett's abduction not related to Devin's?

Was he looking for a desperate father willing to do whatever it took to keep his son?

Or was he looking for someone with more sinister plans for the young boys?

What he wouldn't give to have an answer to those questions.

"How long until …" he trailed off when he saw Mia emerge from the forest with two men behind her carrying a stretcher between them. "Never mind, I see they're here."

With a quick nod at the two men, Julian hurried over to meet Mia as they crossed the clearing toward the waiting ambulance. As he got closer, he noticed immediately that something was wrong. Mia didn't look injured, but a stiffness about her told him she was on edge. She'd been on edge the other day too, something was obviously going on with her, but since they weren't together any longer, it really wasn't his place to ferret it out of her.

Didn't stop him from wanting to find out the problem and fix it though.

"Julian," she said with a smile. He noticed some of the tension left her body, and he felt something deep inside him relax. Despite the fact that he had broken her trust in the worst possible way, she seemed to still have faith in him.

"Everything okay?" he asked, doing a visual sweep of her body just in case he had missed an injury that could be the cause of her apparent anxiety.

"Fine," she said. Her voice was calm and controlled, her face an impassive mask of professionalism, and yet her declaration did nothing to ease his conviction that something had upset her. "Parker is stable but will be transported to the hospital for blood work and to be monitored until he wakes up."

As she spoke the door to the search and rescue base's main building was flung open, and Parker's family came rushing out, running—sobbing—toward the stretcher that had continued toward the ambulance while he and Mia had stood talking.

"At least they got him back alive," Mia said, her gaze fixed on the little family as she worried her bottom lip with her teeth.

"They were lucky, but the next family might not be."

Mia's gaze flew to his, her green eyes filled with worry. "You think there'll be a next time?"

"I don't know enough yet to make that determination, but I'll be going forward under the assumption that it's likely."

"But I thought that Devin's dad was the one who took him."

"That's what we thought, but this puts a kink in that theory. Doesn't mean that it wasn't Vince," he added when Mia paled at his words. "CSU didn't find anything useful where Devin was found, and I'm doubtful they'll find anything this time either." Julian didn't have to ask to know that Mia would have taken photos and marked off the area so CSU could find it easily, he already knew she would have done both. "Assuming that Parker was also drugged with Rohypnol, it's unlikely that he's going to remember anything which means that you are the best source of information we have right now."

"Me?" Her eyes grew wide, and she bit on her bottom lip hard enough that he was afraid she was going to break through the skin.

He reached out a hand to touch her, comfort her, but then hesitated, unsure that she would want his comfort. His hand hovered between them, lost in no man's land. He couldn't help but stare at it, wishing he could take the last two seconds back, Mia also stared at his hand, but the expression on her face didn't give anything away.

Well, this was awkward.

Julian let his hand drop, and when he looked up he could have sworn that he saw disappointment on her face.

Before he could rethink things, he reached out and grabbed her hand, squeezing once before letting go. As he went to release her, Mia curled her fingers around his, holding on.

Surprised, he looked from their joined hands to Mia's face, not wanting to read more to this than she intended. Perhaps she just needed reassurance right now, and he was the only one here to offer it.

He hated this.

It felt like being back in middle school again, obsessing over hand-holding and full of uncertainties about their relationship. That was the opposite of how his relationship with Mia had already been, they'd always had a connection, and it had always seemed so simple, so easy. Then one man's obsession had changed everything.

Her hand was small in his, and cold, and he automatically reached for her other hand, sandwiching both between his and rubbing them to warm them. When her big green eyes met his, and the tip of her tongue darted out to wet her bottom lip, he had to fight his automatic response to drag her up against him and kiss her.

Instead, he kept her hands between his and did his best to focus on this case, for the moment that had to be his focus. "Mia, you're the one who found both boys, the first one at both of the crime scenes, right now, you're the best thing I have."

That was a loaded comment if ever there was one.

Julian had meant it in regards to this case, but it was true.

Mia was always the best thing that had ever happened to him. They connected on a level he only knew was possible because of Mia, she was a part of him, she was his heart and his soul, and loving her was as natural as breathing.

Tentatively, he reached up and cupped her cheek in his hand, letting his fingertips gently caress her soft skin.

He'd missed her.

Missed her with a soul deep ache.

She was watching him intently, there was the same confusion he felt reflected back in her eyes, but when her gaze dropped to his lips, he knew that she wanted this too.

Keeping one hand on her face, his other arm snaked around her waist, pulling her against him. Her hands rested on his chest, her body molded as closely against his as it could be while they were both fully clothed. A soft sigh escaped her lips, and she leaned into him.

With a feeling of coming home, Julian captured her lips with his, kissing her chastely given they were both supposed to be working.

He held her for a moment longer, drinking in the feel of her body in his arms again like she was an oasis in the desert.

Reluctantly, he released her and took a step back because he knew without a shadow of a doubt that if he didn't, she would be back in his arms and they would be doing a whole lot more than kissing, and they couldn't do that here for all the reason he had to remind himself of all over again.

He could have sworn Mia looked disappointed by his distance, but she schooled her features into a professional mask once again. "I'll send you the pictures that I took, but other than that, I don't really know what to tell you. Parker looked just like Devin did when I found him, lying on his back, under a tree, hands folded and resting on his stomach."

"All right, well if you think of anything else you'll let me know?"

"Of course."

"Same deal as last time, I'm going to need your clothes to send to the lab in case any evidence transferred from Parker to you." Knowing that she was about to go inside and undress had him picturing the two of them together in the bedroom, him removing each piece of her clothing slowly as he kissed his way across every part of her body, a body he knew every inch of. Each scar, each freckle, he had long ago memorized them, and if he didn't stop thinking about the little gasping pants she made when she was close to coming, and the way her body shuddered with release, he was going to have to walk out of here with the evidence of his desire for her sticking out for everyone to see.

"I'll have my clothes in a bag ready for CSU to take with them," Mia said.

"I'd still like to talk to you later, go through everything with you slowly, make sure there wasn't anything you saw or heard that might be relevant," he said, and definitely not because he was after an excuse to see her again.

"Sure," she agreed.

"Okay then," he said, the awkwardness back. He wanted to kiss her goodbye but didn't think he could put his hands on her again and not walk away from here without an erection, so he settled for a nod before he turned and headed for his vehicle.

There should be plenty to keep his mind occupied. He would have to go to the hospital, check to find out the results of Parker's blood work, speak with the boy's family to see if there was anyone who might want to hurt them, or anything suspicious they had seen over the last few days. He'd need to speak with Vince Deville again, Parker when he was conscious, CSU, and then his team.

Instead, all he could think of was Mia.

"'Bout time," Lyle muttered under his breath as Julian strode past him. "You know we all lost bets on how long it would take you two to figure things out and get back together, but better late than never."

Julian just rolled his eyes at the old man, but as he climbed back into his car he couldn't help but think Lyle was right. He had let Mia down, they'd wasted eighteen months that they could have enjoyed together, but given their kiss he had to assume that Mia still had feelings for him, so maybe it was time.

Better late than never.

\* \* \* \* \*

10:40 A.M.

"Mia," Eileen sing-songed.

"Be there in a minute," she called out as she zipped up her jeans, flushed the toilet, and came out to wash her hands.

Apparently, whatever it was couldn't wait because her friend was standing in the doorway with a big grin on her pretty face. Eileen was about the same age as her, just a year older, and had large brown eyes framed by the longest lashes Mia had ever seen and straight brown hair that hung to her bottom. She was bubbly, bright, and full of energy, and she loved to talk to the point that Mia sometimes had to gently send her into another room so she could get some work done. As far as she knew, Eileen didn't have any family, but the woman didn't like to talk about her personal life much. What they usually talked about was Mia's personal life.

Or lack thereof.

Although maybe that was about to change.

Julian had kissed her, although they hadn't spoken about if that meant anything and he still hadn't told her what was going on inside his head. Something they had argued about a lot when he was deployed. He hadn't wanted to share anything with her of the horrors he had witnessed, but she had known it was taking a toll on him, holding it all in, and while she didn't need details she wanted him to know that it was safe to tell her anything.

That was totally the pot calling the kettle black though, because when she was the one who had lived through horrors most people couldn't even imagine, she hadn't been forthcoming at all about what was going on inside her head.

"What's going on?" she asked after she'd dried her hands and crossed the locker room. She knew it wasn't anything bad because Eileen couldn't wipe the grin off her face and was practically bouncing from foot to foot.

"Flower, for you." Eileen grinned, holding out a single long-stemmed white rose that had been wrapped in soft white tissue paper.

"It's beautiful," she gushed as she took the flower and touched a fingertip to the delicate petals.

"Your boyfriend is really stepping up his game." Eileen gave an approving nod.

"He's not my boyfriend," she said as she headed for the

kitchen to stick this in the vase with the bluebells from the other day.

"Not your boyfriend? Then why is he leaving you flowers?" Eileen asked, clearly confused as she trailed along behind her.

"It's a long and complicated story," Mia said, not wanting to rehash it all because it was still too raw and painful.

"You can talk to me." Eileen placed a comforting hand on her shoulder and gave a small squeeze. "I'm here for you. I mean, I know you have other friends that you can talk to, but I wanted you to know I'm here too."

Mia turned and gave her friend a warm smile. Although Eileen had settled into River's End pretty smoothly she still kept to herself a little, even if she was the life of the party when she was around. "That means a lot to me, it really does. Julian and I, well, technically we're still married, but ..."

"Married?" Eileen squealed. "You never told me you were married."

"Well, like I said it's only a technicality. We filled out the divorce papers, but ..."

Eileen held up a hand. "Okay, we need coffee."

"And chocolate," Mia added as she arranged the rose in the middle of the vase then dragged a chair over to the refrigerator so she could access the cupboard above it. Hidden in the back was her emergency stash of chocolate.

Once they were both sitting at the table, mugs of coffee in front of them, chocolate divided between them, Eileen looked at her expectantly. "Shoot."

"Well, as I was saying, Julian and I separated about six months before you moved to River's End. I filed for divorce, and he signed the papers, but for some reason, I couldn't file them so they're still sitting in my desk draw at home."

"How long were you two together?"

"Since junior high."

"And what happened? Why did you split up?"

"I had a stalker who after months of leaving me flowers and gifts, and contacting me, decided he had waited long enough. He kidnapped me, dragged me out into the forest, he sexually assaulted me, but I managed to get ahold of his gun and killed him. I wandered through the forest, lost and bleeding for a while, and eventually Julian and my team found me. I was pretty messed up afterward."

"Understandably," Eileen inserted.

Mia nodded. "I couldn't deal with killing him, he was sick he needed help, and it just ate away at me. I shut down, and eventually Julian had enough, and he left."

Eileen's brows knitted together in a frown. "He just up and left you after you went through all that?"

"He didn't just up and leave," Mia protested, driven by an innate need to defend Julian. "He tried to help me, did everything he could, begged me to get help, but I had shut down. I think him leaving was his way of trying to give me a wake-up call. The day he packed his bags and left I broke down. My dad came over to find me sobbing hysterically on the bed, he didn't take no for an answer and drove me straight to see a therapist. It helped a lot, and over the last year and a half I rebuilt my life. Well, most of it anyway."

"But you still miss him," Eileen said, a statement not a question, but she nodded anyway.

"Yeah, I still miss him."

"So you're getting back together?"

"I don't know."

"He sent you flowers, that sounds like a boyfriend—husband—thing to do."

"But he hasn't asked me out, hasn't told me he still loves me or that he still cares, hasn't told me anything at all." Which left her feeling confused and uncertain, it felt like Julian was giving her mixed signals. He'd left her flowers three times, and he'd kissed her outside earlier, but he hadn't spoken, and she didn't see how they could move forward without talking through their issues. If they tried to, it seemed like just setting themselves up to fail, and the last thing either of them needed was more pain.

"That leaves you feeling vulnerable," Eileen said astutely.

"Yeah, it does," she acknowledged. It left her feeling like all of those wounds which had only just scabbed over were simply waiting for a nail to come and scratch them off.

Her phone rang, and absently, she slipped it out of her pocket. "Hello?" she said without checking to see the name on the screen.

"Hey, Mia-bug."

She sucked in a breath as the nickname registered before the deep timbre of his voice. "Julian."

"The one and only."

Before she could let her hopes start growing wings and flying high, she kept her tone neutral as she asked, "Did you need to ask me something about the case?"

"Nope."

"Then what do you want?"

"To ask you out."

"O-on a d-date?" she stammered, suddenly feeling like she was every bit the thirteen-year-old girl she had been when he'd asked her out that first time. She'd only ever gone out with one boy before Julian, and she'd been twelve so that had consisted of only going on group dates with all of their friends to see a movie, or go ice skating, or swimming in the river. She hadn't cared about that boy, he'd just been a friend, and she'd said yes when he asked her out only because she was annoyed that Julian hadn't asked her to go to the Valentine's Day dance at school.

But this was Julian, and there was so much history, so much pain to be suffered if this didn't work out, and she didn't have nervous butterflies in her stomach she had nervous t-rexes stomping about in there.

"Mia?"

"Yeah, I'm here," she said in a small voice.

"So breakfast tomorrow morning?" he asked tentatively, and that uncertainty in his voice hit her firmly in the gut.

He was scared too.

They were both nervous about this, and the only reason she could think of that he would be so unsure was that he was as invested in them as she still was.

They both knew the stakes, both knew they couldn't survive another blow like the one Joshua had delivered, while both also knowing that what they had was a once in a lifetime kind of love.

She had needed a sign, needed to know what Julian wanted before she could figure out what she wanted, but now it was all so clear.

"I would love to go out to breakfast with you tomorrow."

"Perfect," he said, and she could hear in his tone that a weight had been lifted off his shoulders. "I'll pick you up at seven."

"I'll be waiting. I'm looking forward to it."

"Me too, sweetheart, me too," Julian said.

As she hung up her phone she felt like her world just got a little closer to righting its axis.

\* \* \* \* \*

3:27 P.M.

Two kidnapped little boys, both drugged with Rohypnol and left in identical circumstances in the forest. Julian knew that that should be enough to keep a smile off his face and yet he knew he was grinning like an idiot.

How could he not?

Mia had said yes.

Part of him had been sure she was going to say no when he asked her out. It had been Lyle's words that motivated him to call. Better late than never. That saying had repeated itself in his brain as he drove to the hospital. When he boiled down all the uncertainties and guilt and fear, there was only one thing that mattered.

He loved Mia.

That hadn't changed, and they had wasted enough time being apart. He was willing to risk his heart for the woman who owned it anyway.

It hadn't been his since he was thirteen, it had belonged to Mia so when he looked at it that way there really wasn't any other option.

Still, he hadn't been sure she would accept. Things between them were so messed up, so far from what he wanted, and right now it was hard to see a way to get back to what they'd had before, but he had to have hope.

Because living without Mia wasn't really living at all.

It was going to be a long night, and he was probably going to obsess over the date more than a thirty-year-old man who had served a tour in the Marines should, but he wasn't a rational human being when it came to Mia.

A car pulled up into the driveway and Julian climbed out of his truck, shoving thoughts of Mia to the back of his mind. There would be time to think—obsess—about her later, but right now he was here to do his job.

"You again," Vince growled when he caught sight of him walking across the front lawn. "Thanks to you, Lacey won't even let me see Devin. You put this idea in her head that I'm this monster who would kidnap and drug his own son."

"I didn't put that idea in her head, Vince, she's the one who suggested you as a suspect," he said calmly.

"You ever think that *she* was the one who had a reason to be afraid of losing Devin?" Vince demanded. "I would have gotten joint custody, there was no reason for me not to. She was the one who would have had to share him. She was used to being the one in control. Joint legal custody meant that I got to be a part of the day-to-day life of my son. Lacey was the one in charge and the one with something to lose when I got joint custody. Maybe she was the one who kidnapped Devin or paid someone else to do it for her."

They had already looked into Lacey Deville because they looked into everyone when it came to the abduction of a child. However, Lacey had an ironclad alibi when Devin went missing. She had given them permission to look into her financials. There was nothing suspicious, nothing suggesting that she had paid someone to abduct her son.

Since he was here to get information not to hand it out, Julian ignored Vince's attempt to throw his ex-wife under the bus and instead asked his own question. "Where have you been today, Vince?"

"I went to Lacey's to see Devin."

"That was at lunchtime," he reminded the other man. After checking in on Parker at the hospital, he'd been called over to Lacey's house when a call had come in reporting a disturbance. The disturbance had been Lacey who, afraid that Vince was the one who had kidnapped Devin, had refused to let him into the house and Vince had lost it. It had taken Julian a while to calm her down and recommended that she go and take out a temporary restraining order preventing Vince from coming within a hundred yards of either her, Devin, or their house. While he'd been consoling Lacey, Vince had disappeared, he'd been waiting here for over an hour now for the man to return home.

Since Vince hadn't arrived at Lacey's until lunchtime there was the entire morning unaccounted for. Plenty of time for the man to have abducted Parker, left him in the forest, then hung around to make sure the boy was found before heading to his ex's house.

"I had some stuff to do this morning." Vince huffed, unable to make eye contact.

"What stuff?"

"Why?" The man looked up and glared.

"Parker Barrett was abducted this morning," Julian announced, watching closely to gauge Vince's reaction.

His eyes narrowed. "What's that got to do with me?"

"Parker is around the same age as Devin, he was grabbed on his way to school, found in the forest, only ten miles from where Devin was found. Both boys had been drugged with Rohypnol and left lying under a tree with their hands on their stomachs. You know what we call that, Vince? We call that an MO."

"Me?" Vince sputtered. "You think I didn't just abduct my own kid, but someone else's too? Why would I do that? Tell me on what planet that makes any sense at all? Okay, I can see why you *might* think that I tried to take Devin if I thought I was going to lose him, but what would kidnapping Parker Barrett achieve?"

"It would theoretically point the finger away from you."

"What?"

"Let's go with the theory that you were the one who took Devin. You backed out either because you were afraid of getting caught or you couldn't go through with it. Then you find out that the cops are onto you, you're the number one suspect, and you have to think of a way to turn the heat down, point us in a new direction. So you decide that two missing kids means that it wasn't necessarily personal, but just someone after little boys. Taking Parker makes it look like we have someone in town targeting the children, rather than a desperate father resorting to desperate measures to get what he wants."

Vince snorted. "That's ridiculous. I didn't take my boy, and I certainly didn't touch Parker Barrett."

"Then tell me where you were this morning. You say that you love your son, that you rearranged your life so that you could be around for him more often and share physical custody, and yet when I told you yesterday about what happened to Devin you didn't go straight to see him. Instead, you waited until lunchtime today. Why, Vince? Help me understand." As far as he was concerned, the fact that Vince had delayed seeing Devin was further proof that he was involved. Maybe he was afraid that if he saw Devin again too soon that the boy's memories might come back and he might recall something incriminating.

"I wasn't anywhere, just here." Vince huffed.

"So why not go and see Devin right away? Why wait?"

Vince shuffled from foot to foot, staring at the ground then finally looking up to meet his gaze. "I was afraid, okay?"

"Of what?"

"Of what happened when I went to Lacey's. I was scared she was going to freak out and do exactly what she did. You think it's me, but I swear I didn't do anything to Devin or Parker. You should be looking at Lacey, look how quickly she spat out my name, got you off her trail and focused on me, but I keep telling you I had no reason to take Devin. I was going to get joint custody, she was the one with something to lose not me, and now she has you focused on me, and she's using it to shove me out of my son's life."

Anger had Vince's cheeks turning red, and Julian had to admit that there was some merit to what Vince was saying. They would take another look at Lacey Deville to see if there was anything they had missed, but that didn't mean that Vince was no longer a suspect.

"I promise you that we will look into everything. If you are the one who took Devin and Parker, then I'll make sure you serve the maximum sentence in prison. But if it was Lacey, or anyone else, then I'll also make sure that they get the max. We're not looking for a scapegoat, Vince, we're looking for the perpetrator. Word of warning though, if you're telling the truth don't go and do anything stupid. If Lacey did this then let me do my job and prove it. If you go and try to take matters into your own hands you're only going to make things worse. And if you were the one who did it, do yourself a favor and turn yourself in, the longer you try to hide and the more you lie, the bigger the hole you're digging yourself into."

Having delivered his warning, he left Vince to consider

everything he had said and headed off to dig deeper into this case to find the answers he needed. No more little boys were going missing on his watch.

# OCTOBER 7TH

Mia gave herself a critical once over in the bathroom mirror. She'd put on a little makeup, more than she usually would when going to work, but not as much as she would usually use for a date. Her hair was in a simple ponytail, and she was wearing just jeans and a long sleeve t-shirt, her typical work attire, but she wished she could dress up, make this feel like a real date instead of just a quick breakfast before they both went to work.

At least a breakfast date was less pressure than a dinner date.

There would be no possibility of making out after the date, no standing on the doorstep wondering if they were going to kiss or if anything more was going to happen. At most, this date would end with a kiss. No doubt a chaste one like the one outside her work yesterday.

She wanted more.

So much more.

There was no use pretending otherwise, although she still had reservations about this whole getting back with Julian idea, it was what her heart wanted. Her brain however was going to need some convincing.

Her doorbell rang, and she frowned at herself. She might not look the way she wanted for a date, but it was what it was. There was no point getting all dressed up only to have to come back here and change later. Besides, this was just a first date and a breakfast one at that. It was supposed to be less pressure, and she was sure that was why Julian had chosen to ask her out for

64

breakfast instead of dinner.

Determined not to overanalyze that, Mia switched off the light and ran downstairs, grabbing her purse on the way. When she opened the front door she couldn't stop her mouth from dropping open. How did Julian manage to make jeans and a t-shirt look so sexy? Here she was feeling like a pre-teen heading off to play in the forest, and there was Julian, dressed almost the same as she was, looking like he was off for a model photoshoot.

"You look beautiful," Julian said, causing her gaze to snap up to meet his.

Surely he was joking.

"I wear this every day to work, in fact I was wearing this yesterday, only this long sleeve t-shirt is green, not purple."

"You looked beautiful yesterday, too," he said. "Mia, you look gorgeous every day."

She rolled her eyes, but inside a little flicker of pleasure lit. Some days she didn't feel beautiful. Some days she still felt like she had that day she had killed Joshua and wandered through the forest, injured, dirty, disoriented, and covered in both her blood and his. Some days it was hard to let go of the sense of filthiness that her ordeal had left her with. Some days it seemed so ingrained that she could never be clean, never be free of it.

"Sweetheart?" Julian asked as he reached out and gently took her chin between his thumb and forefinger, tilting her face up to look at him. "What are you thinking about that took that smile off your pretty face?"

Determined not to let Joshua Graves take anything else away from her, she shoved all thoughts of her stalker aside and focused on Julian. "It's nothing. You ready to go?"

His hazel eyes studied hers for a moment, concern shining brightly, but then he released her chin and took her hand, entwining their fingers as he walked her down the garden path to the street where his car was waiting. "I thought I'd drive you to breakfast then drop you off here so you can pick up your car to go to work."

"That seems like extra work for you. I can drive myself to breakfast."

"Driving you means I get extra time with you," Julian told her in a voice that said he had already made up his mind and arguing was futile.

And to be honest, she didn't want to argue anyway. She wasn't going to say no to a little extra time with Julian, and that he wanted those couple of extra minutes with her made a pleasurable flush sweep through her body.

In the car, they settled into a companionable silence and Mia took the opportunity to study the face she knew so well, but that had felt like a stranger's these last eighteen months. His strong jaw was covered in a little more stubble than it used to be, and there were a few new lines around his eyes that hadn't been there before. He was wearing his hair a little shorter than it had been when they'd been together, and she spied a new tattoo peeking out under the sleeve of his gray t-shirt.

She'd missed him.

She hadn't even realized how much until this very moment.

Could they really do this? Could they really find their way back to one another?

Julian parked in front of the diner and came around to open her door for her, taking her hand as soon as she was out of the car.

"You know within the next ten minutes, everyone in River's End is going to know that we were seen holding hands and having breakfast together."

"I think that kiss yesterday already clued everyone in," he said and his eyes heated in a way that said he currently wished they didn't have an audience so they could do a replay on that kiss.

"They're going to think we're back together," she said and felt Julian freeze.

"There a problem with that?" he demanded, looking down at

her.

Was there?

Her heart said no, but her brain said yes. She wanted to work out their issues without having the pressure of everyone expecting them to have already done it and be past them and a couple again. Just because she didn't solely blame Julian for what had happened, it didn't mean that she was prepared to just jump headfirst back into a relationship.

No.

She had to be smart.

She couldn't go through losing him a second time.

"Mia, I want you back," Julian said, curling an arm around her waist to draw her closer. "I'm not here to play games, I'm not here to waste your time, I'm here because I love you."

Some of her doubts melted away now that she knew exactly what Julian wanted. "I love you too," she said, pressing her face against his chest and breathing in the scent she had missed so deeply. For weeks after Julian had moved out, she'd slept with an old t-shirt of his he'd left behind in the bed with her. She'd needed it to try to keep the nightmares at bay.

They stayed that way, holding onto each other in the middle of the street until her stomach chose that moment to let out a loud rumble.

Julian laughed. "Come on, sweetheart, let's go get you some breakfast."

Taking his hand, they walked inside the diner and chose a quiet booth in the back so they could have a little privacy.

"What are you having?" Julian asked her.

"Pancakes," she said without hesitation. Those had been a favorite of hers for as long as she could remember.

"Henry makes the best pancakes, after your dad's," Julian said.

Her smile faltered at the mention of her father. He wasn't doing well. After they'd talked about Julian the other night, she finally managed to get him to give her a proper update on his health. According to his doctor, he had months left at best. She was desperate to convince him to move in with her so she could look after him as his health continued to decline, and spend as much of the time he had left with her, but so far he was still stubbornly refusing.

"Hey, what's wrong?" Julian asked, his large hand covering hers.

Drawing strength from his touch, Mia made herself say the words out loud for the first time. "He's dying. He didn't respond to treatment, and he decided to stop. He said he doesn't want to spend the limited time he has left being sick and in a hospital."

"Oh, sweetheart." Julian slid out of his side of the booth and joined her on her side, sliding her onto his lap.

Any embarrassment she might have felt from being cradled on his lap in the middle of the diner was chased away by the comfort she felt from being wrapped up in his arms.

"How long do they think he has?" Julian asked.

"Months, if we're lucky maybe six or more, but it could be as little as only a month. I'm not ready, Julian," she admitted. "When he goes I'll be all alone, I won't have a family anymore."

"Hey now, that's not true. You'll have me, and you have my family, my dad, my aunt and uncle, my brother, and cousins, and all their wives and girlfriends, they all love you and consider you family."

Mia knew that was true, and she loved every member of the Black family, but it wasn't the same. If this didn't work out with Julian, then they would be his family, not hers, and she would be left out in the cold, alone.

"No, sweetheart, you won't ever be alone. Not ever. It's just not possible because, like it or not, our lives are so entwined that they can't ever be separated. We tried, we let Joshua ruin what we had, and let our own issues and fears drive a wedge between us, but it didn't work. I can't stay away from you. I love you, Mia, and my love for you only grows with each passing day."

His sweet words were the last straw. A sob tore through her chest and then she was weeping freely, her face buried in Julian's neck as she cried for all the losses she'd suffered and the ones that were still to come.

\* \* \* \* \*

7:11 A.M.

Julian held Mia while she cried. One hand kept her tucked snugly against him while his other stroked her back and rubbed circles, anything to try to soothe her.

"It's okay, baby, get it all out," he murmured in her ear. "I've got you, you're not alone, sweetheart, I'm here. I'm right here. I got you." He whispered a string of consolations in her ear, oblivious to the diner's other patrons, his attention focused solely on the woman in his lap.

Mia cried for a few more minutes, then sunk heavily against him as though physically spent of energy. They stayed that way for several more minutes until she roused herself and placed her hands on his chest to ease herself up.

"Sorry for crying all over you," she said, indicating the wet patch on his t-shirt. That was the last thing he cared about right now.

"Feel better?" he asked as he caught a stray tear still tumbling down her cheek with the pad of his thumb.

"Yeah, actually I do. I haven't cried about Dad's diagnosis yet. I guess I wanted to try to not make it seem real, but saying out loud to you that I'm going to lose him soon just made all those emotions I'd been trying to keep shoved down bubble up."

"You shouldn't do that, Mia," he reprimanded gently. Shoving her emotions into a box and keeping them locked away was one of the issues that had led to them breaking up.

"I love him so much. I don't want to lose him, I want to be

able to stop it from happening, and knowing that I can't is killing me," she admitted. "I try to stay positive for him, upbeat, I don't want him to worry about me when he's gone."

"But doing that is taking a toll on you." It was evident in the dark circles under her eyes, her cheekbones which were a little too pronounced, indicating she'd lost weight, and there was a deep sadness etched into every millimeter of her face.

"Better me than him."

"My sweet, strong, Mia," he said, taking her face in his hands and kissing her forehead. "I worry about you."

"I know. I hate it."

"That's what you do when you love someone and they're hurting."

"I know, but I still don't like it." She offered him a half-smile, and he felt her body start to relax.

Before he could say anything else his phone began to ring.

Disappointment was a heavy weight on his chest when he met her gaze. "Sorry, I have to take this."

Mia was already sliding off his lap as he spoke. "I remember the drill."

That she looked and sounded as disappointed as he felt eased away some of the annoyance at getting called away because at least Mia was as invested in this as he was.

Keeping an arm around her as she sat beside him, he pulled out his phone and answered. "What's up?"

"We got another one," Fletcher Harris told him. Fletcher was one of the other deputies in River's End and had been best friends with his cousin Theo since the two of them were small boys. He was practically part of the family as was Fletcher's sister Florence and her husband Eli who lived in Manhattan but made frequent visits to the small town she had grown up in.

"Another abduction?" he asked, looking at Mia who hadn't received a phone call. If another boy was missing in the forests surrounding River's End, she would have been called in too as the head of search and rescue.

"We think so. Rowan Douglas was grabbed on his way to school, but the abduction was foiled," Fletcher explained.

"So we have our guy?"

"No, he managed to get away in the resulting hullabaloo."

"Hullabaloo?" he couldn't not ask.

"It seemed to fit the situation."

Julian laughed. "Okay, then. Did we at least get a license plate or a description of the guy?"

"Unfortunately, no."

"Then how did the abduction get derailed if whoever did the derailing didn't get a good look at the guy or his car?"

"It was the two old Miss Salsburys that were the ones who saw it happen," Fletcher informed him.

Eva and Evelyn Salsbury were both in their late eighties. Neither had married, and they had lived together since they both retired—Eva from a lifetime traveling the globe as a photographer, and Evelyn from her work as an accountant—nearly two decades ago. Both women were well known and well liked around town, and could usually be spotted walking about or standing on someone's front lawn chattering away. It was no wonder the two had been out despite the early hour, nor was it a wonder that they hadn't hesitated to intervene despite their age.

"All right, I'm on my way," he said on a sigh.

"Sorry to interrupt your date with Mia."

"How did you know I'm on a date with Mia?"

"Mia told her friends, each of whom told their guys, all of whom have blabbed it to me," Fletcher said with a laugh.

"Gossips," he muttered. He didn't mind the whole world knowing that they were trying to work things out, but it seemed to bother Mia which meant it bothered him too.

"We're on Berry Street," Fletcher told him before disconnecting the call.

"Another boy was abducted?" Mia asked the second he

removed his phone from his ear.

"Attempted. The Miss Salsburys intervened and were able to stop Rowan Douglas from being taken."

Her eyes grew wide. "Are they okay? Rowan and the Miss Salsburys?"

"Fletcher didn't mention any injuries," he assured her. "But …"

"You have to leave," she finished for him. "I remember, Julian, I really do. Just because River's End is a small town and we usually don't have a lot of crime, sometimes your job means you have to leave at a moment's notice, and sometimes at the most inopportune times."

"Thanks for understanding."

"I always did."

"Yeah, you did," he agreed. Leaning down, he gave her a much quicker kiss than the one he had intended on giving her at the end of the date, then pulled out a twenty and left it on the table. "Breakfast is still my treat."

Before Mia could protest, he was already heading for the door. It wasn't until he was in his car and driving that he realized he hadn't rescheduled their date. That they would be going out again was a given as far as he was concerned, but he still had to make that official. As soon as he had a handle on what had happened this morning, he would call Mia and set something up.

As soon as he reached Berry Street, he saw the hullabaloo. Fletcher's department car was on the scene, as was an ambulance, and there were almost two dozen people gathered in small groups on the sidewalk gawking at what was going on.

The crowd parted for him as he headed for where Eva and Evelyn Salsbury were standing. Fletcher nodded at him and then at the ambulance he was standing beside, indicating he would follow it to the hospital and Julian could meet him there once he finished talking to their witnesses.

"I see you two played hero this morning," he said as he joined the two old women.

"You're never too old to make a difference in the world," Eva said with a smile that couldn't hide the worry in her brown eyes.

"Can you tell me exactly what you saw?" he asked.

"We heard about the other abductions, little Devin Deville and Parker Barrett," Evelyn explained. "So we knew as soon as we saw it that something was wrong."

"Saw what exactly?"

"Someone holding Rowan Douglas," Eva replied.

"Holding him like you would a baby," Evelyn added, miming holding someone in your outstretched arms.

"Rowan is a tiny little thing, but there should be no reason that you would be holding him like that," Eva continued. "So we knew something was wrong."

"Was Rowan fighting whoever was holding him?"

"No, he was just lying there, all limp-like," Eva answered.

"And one thing a small boy isn't is docile," Evelyn said.

That was certainly true. He remembered what he and his brother and cousins had been like as little boys. They had been like a mass of little tornados who got into everything and were always on the move. The would-be kidnapper had obviously already drugged Rowan by the time the Miss Salsburys had seen him and was ready to put him in the car and leave. "So, what did you do?"

"We screamed," Eva said simply. "Fire, help, whatever we could think of, and people started coming out of their houses."

"That was when he put Rowan down and jumped into a car and sped off down the street," Evelyn said.

"Where were you and where were Rowan and the man?" he asked.

"We were just back there." Eva pointed to the McKinnly house about six houses back from where they were standing. "And Rowan was right there." She pointed to the spot where the ambulance had just taken off from.

"Can you give me anything on the would-be kidnapper?" he asked. He knew both women were old and had poor eyesight, but he wanted something that would help him identify this man before he went after another boy.

"Tall," Eva said.

"He was wearing a bright blue beanie," Evelyn added.

"Maybe jeans and a black jacket," Eva said but didn't look certain.

"And the car? Can you describe it?"

"Big," Evelyn said.

"A truck," Eva added.

"It was gray," Evelyn said.

Eva frowned. "I think it was white."

"Are you both comfortable saying it was light in color?" he asked, it wasn't much but it would at least narrow things down.

"Yes," the sisters said in unison.

"Anything else you can think of that you want to tell me?"

"Only that we hope you catch him," Eva said fiercely, her sister nodding vigorously.

"Okay, ladies, thank you so much for what you did for Rowan."

Evelyn waved off his words. "Wasn't anything any decent sort of folk wouldn't have done."

Thanking the women again, Julian headed to his car, ready to drive to the hospital and find out if Rowan had also been drugged with Rohypnol. Three boys in four days, all snatched right off the streets in their quiet little town. Whether they were looking at Vince Deville, Lacey, or someone else, it was clear they were going to have to issue a warning that no boys be allowed to go anywhere alone. So far none of the children had been physically harmed, but there was no guarantee that was going to last.

\* \* \* \* \*

74

8:02 A.M.

Mia was just setting down her knife and fork when she glanced up to see a swarm descending on her.

Okay, so maybe a swarm wasn't the best way to describe her friends, but she wasn't in the mood for the interrogation she knew was coming.

She felt empty.

Drained.

Her dad's illness, this thing with Julian, the creepy feeling of being watched on the last two searches, everything was catching up with her all at once, and she needed some time to process.

"Where's Julian?" Renee asked as she dropped down onto the bench beside her.

"He had to leave," Mia replied.

"Another boy was almost taken," Sydney explained. "It's supposed to be my day off today, but Abe called me to tell me to come in at lunchtime. It's all hands on deck until we get this guy off the streets."

At least Rowan hadn't been taken out into the forest, Mia wasn't sure her nerves could handle another search right now. Which annoyed her as much as bothered her, she was sure these imaginary eyes she kept feeling watching her were just a reaction to the stress of knowing that her time left with her dad was limited. She was afraid of being left alone, and her brain was manifesting that fear in the feeling of constantly being watched and not alone.

"So, how did the date go?" Poppy asked as she nudged Renee over and sat on the last space on Mia's side of the booth as Sydney, Maggie, and Meadow took the bench on the other side of the table.

"Since I'm here eating breakfast alone I think you can figure that out," she replied. She didn't mean to sound so snappy and grumpy, but she couldn't seem to help herself.

Her friends exchanged glances before Maggie asked, "So things between you two aren't a go?"

"I don't know," she said simply, staring at her plate. After Julian had left, she'd decided she couldn't eat pancakes because they were going to make her start crying again so she'd settled on waffles. They were delicious, but she hadn't been able to taste them as she forced them down, her mind attempting to run in a million different directions at once.

"You don't sound very enthusiastic about the idea," Meadow noted.

"I know you felt like you needed to know what Julian wanted before you could figure out what you wanted. Did he not give you any indication of what it is he wants from you?" Poppy asked.

"He said that he wants us to get back together," she replied.

"And the problem is?" Renee asked after a minute passed and she didn't offer any more information.

"Is that not what you want? Do you not love him anymore?" Meadow asked.

"No," she said adamantly. She would love Julian Black until the day she died whether they were a couple or not. "I've always loved Julian, and nothing has changed."

"Do you blame him for what happened?" Maggie asked.

"Because he blames himself," Poppy added, and Maggie nodded. Of her group of friends, only Maggie and Poppy had been in River's End when everything went down with her stalker. Both Meadow and Sydney had only moved to town this year, and while Renee had grown up here, she had only recently moved back.

"I know he does," she said in a small voice. That had been one of the worst things to deal with, Julian's guilt. He was a cop, they had known she had a stalker, and he had blamed himself for not protecting her and keeping her safe. In his mind, if he had been a better husband, a better cop, then she would never have been taken, sexually assaulted, shot, and forced to take a life. "I don't blame him, I never did. It wasn't Julian's fault. It was mine. I was the one who didn't take things seriously enough. I didn't think my stalker would be a physical threat to me. I underestimated Joshua and how delusional and determined he was. That is all on me."

"No," Sydney corrected firmly. "That's all on him. I've heard enough about what happened to know that you had no reason to believe he was suddenly going to make a grab for you. All he had done was send gifts and make phone calls, none of which indicated the level of violence he was capable of. What happened wasn't your fault, and it wasn't Julian's fault, it was all Joshua's."

She had heard those same words so many times before, but she was yet to have them fully sink in, and she was sure Julian was the same.

Which was the problem.

"So, if you still love him, and you don't blame him for the stalker, do you blame him for leaving? Can you not forgive him for that?" Renee asked. "Because that is something I understand."

Renee and Will had been in a similar situation to her and Julian. Renee had been attacked, Will had made a bad decision in the aftermath, and it had resulted in the two of them breaking up. It wasn't until Renee came back to town to housesit for her mother that the two of them had reconciled.

"No, well yes and no, I would be lying if I said it didn't hurt, but I know that I was partly to blame for him leaving. I wouldn't deal with anything, I shut down. He tried everything he could to get me to seek help, and I think him leaving was his way of forcing my hand."

"So, what's the problem?" Maggie asked, clearly confused.

"The problem is that nothing has changed," she replied. "We are both still dealing with our issues individually, we haven't talked about anything yet, it feels like the elephant in the room that neither of us wants to address, but we have to. How can we have a hope of rebuilding anything if we don't talk about and deal with what drove us apart in the first place?"

"Then have that conversation," Poppy said.

It sounded so simple when someone else said it, but in her head it wasn't anything close to that simple.

"I'm afraid to," she admitted. Saying it out loud was scary, but these were her best friends, and they told each other everything. No secrets were allowed in this group.

"Of what?" Maggie asked.

"Of finding out that nothing has changed. That Julian is always going to battle his guilt, and I'm also going to bottle things up, and that if we try anything we'll fail and I'll be right back here in this place, alone and scared, and unable to move on with my life because I love Julian too much to ever look at another man," she said in a rush. It felt good to get her fears out there instead of letting them fester inside her.

"There's no guarantee that won't happen," Meadow agreed.

"Aren't you guys supposed to be my cheer squad?' she grumbled.

"We are," Sydney said with a small chuckle.

"Which is why we're telling you this," Poppy added.

"Love is all about risks," Renee told her.

"It's jumping out of a plane and trusting the other person to catch you," Poppy said.

"You are the only one at the table who is ever going to go skydiving," she joked weakly.

"You know what I mean," Poppy said.

"Yeah, I know, but I'm scared. I'm not good at taking risks."

"You work search and rescue. Every time you go to work you're risking your life," Sydney reminded her.

"That's different," she protested. "Those are calculated risks. I know what I'm doing, I'm trained to do it, I have everything on my back I would need to survive virtually any situation, and I have a team that I trust. It's not the same."

"Risking your heart is definitely scary," Renee agreed.

"Amen," Sydney added.

"You can still do the same things to make the risk more calculated," Maggie reminded her. "You know yourself, your strengths and weaknesses and struggles, and you know Julian and his strengths and weaknesses and struggles. You know the issues that came between you last time, so you know what to be on the lookout for and how to stop it from happening again. And you know that the rewards if everything works out massively outweigh the negatives. So really it kind of is the same as you do every day with your job."

Mia had never thought about it that way before, she'd always let her fears rule, and maybe that was her biggest obstacle to overcome. She didn't fully trust anyone, not even herself. That was why she felt like she had to keep her life neatly organized and under control. It was why she could do her job but not employ those same principles to her heart.

She hated to be vulnerable, and dealing with a stalker had forced her into that very situation and destabilized her orderly little world.

Her foundation had turned to mush, and she was struggling to rebuild her life, but Julian was strong, confident, reliable, he was just battling his own issues, but maybe together between the two of them they had the tools they both needed to forge new foundations. Better foundations.

It was worth the risk.

Trying meant she might fail, but it also meant she might win.

If it were her work, she would never hold off on a rescue because it might fail. After all, that meant that the person who needed their help was as good as dead already. She took the risk because she trusted her team.

She trusted this team too.

Her friends, and her dad, wouldn't let anything happen to her, they would be there to pick up the pieces if she did fail, and they would celebrate with her if she won, just like her team did when they completed a successful search or rescue.

Julian wanted her, she wanted him, that had to be a pretty good place to start.

\* \* \* \* \*

12:43 P.M.

"Wow, did you guys buy out the whole diner?" Poppy asked as Julian and Beau carried bags filled with food into the precinct.

"Honey, we have five starving guys to feed." Beau teased his girlfriend as he crossed around her desk to give her a kiss. Poppy and her parents had moved to River's End when she was twelve and was pretty much a little sister to Julian and the rest of the guys on the force. After losing her parents earlier in the year, a chance meeting with Detective Beau Caldwell who worked for the Sunnyville police in Southern California, had the two falling in love and Beau transferring here so he could be with Poppy. Although Poppy didn't know it yet, Beau planned to propose to her at the annual Black family Halloween party later this month. Beau had asked everyone to come dressed as brides and grooms, and when Poppy walked in, he was going to drop down onto one knee and propose. It was a sweet and fun idea, and Julian knew Poppy was going to love it.

"So you didn't bring anything for Syd and me?" Poppy arched a brow and tossed her mane of chestnut curls over her shoulder.

"Did I say I was insane?" Beau balked as he set a bag on Poppy's desk, and she punched him in the shoulder. "You better get in there, I think I could hear stomachs growling from out here." Poppy was both the receptionist and office manager at the precinct, and thanks to her, everything was kept running smoothly.

Julian fought back a stab of envy as he watched the happy couple banter, he wanted that same easiness back in his relationship with Mia. He wasn't kidding himself, there was a lot to sort through and a long way to go to get back what they had, but he believed they could do it. He believed they could beat the odds and reconcile.

"Is that food?" Fletcher pounced on them the second they entered the conference room where they worked any bigger cases they got that involved more than just one or two of them working it.

"I'm starving." Will groaned as he took one of the bags from Julian's hand.

"Hey, ladies first, gentlemen," Sydney said as she pushed back her chair and took another of the bags, opening it up and moaning in delight. "I just had one of these sandwiches at the diner this morning. How can I be craving another one already? Oh, Julian, you're going to call Mia to set up another date, right? Because you kind of didn't do that when you rushed out earlier, and she was a little worried you weren't going to."

"What? No, I mean yes, of course I'm going to ask her out again. Why would she think otherwise?"

"Got me." Sydney shrugged as she took her sandwich back to her seat.

"Abe, can I make a call real quick?" he asked his cousin.

"Make it quick," Abe said with a nod.

Stepping out into the corridor where he could get a little privacy, he brought up Mia's name and hit call. She answered on the second ring. "You really thought I wasn't going to ask you out again?" he demanded.

"Well, I uh wasn't sure. You left in a hurry, and I had cried all over you which I'm sure wasn't what you had planned for a good first date, and I didn't know," she finished lamely.

This anxiety and uncertainty they kept feeling when it came to each other had to stop. "Dinner tonight?"

"Oh, I can't tonight," disappointment coated her tone. "I'm having dinner with my dad, and I don't want to cancel on him."

"I would never ask you to. Dinner tomorrow night then?"

"It's a date," she said.

"It's a date," he echoed. "Love you, Mia."

"Love you too."

Grinning, he disconnected the call and went to rejoin the others, who all looked over expectantly when he walked into the room.

"So?" Fletcher prompted.

"So I have a date for tomorrow night."

"About time," Abe muttered as he gestured that Julian should take a seat at the table.

"The timing had to be right," he said, convinced that that was true. The ordeal with Mia's stalker had left them both with scars that had needed to heal a little before they were able to see a way forward.

"We're all happy for you," Sydney said, reaching óver to squeeze his hand.

"We are," Abe said, softening for a moment. "But we have to figure out what's going on in our little town that is supposed to be safe."

"It's not Vince Deville or Lacey," Julian said as he unwrapped his sandwich. "After I went to the hospital to check on Rowan, I went to Lacey's house, found her and Vince there together with Devin. Apparently yesterday, after I finished with Vince, he went over there, managed to keep his cool. The two of them talked, and after listening to Devin say how he felt about them fighting over him, they decided that they were going to try to work something out so everyone was happy. He was still there, spent the night in the guestroom. Devin had nightmares and woke around six, Vince and Lacey were with him, there was no way either of them could have been the one who tried to grab Rowan Douglas. If they're working things out then I don't think there would be any need to continue with this charade, so I think that they're both out as suspects."

"Agreed," Abe said with a single nod. "Any chance that our

theory could have been correct only Devin was a decoy instead of the intended target?"

"Syd and I spoke with Rowan's family and they're happily married with four kids. Rowan is the second oldest, I can't see any reason why one of them would have tried to snatch him and not the other kids," Fletcher explained.

"Beau and I re-interviewed Parker's mom," Will said. "There's no father in the picture, never was, none listed on Parker's birth certificate. Francine works hard to provide for herself and Parker and has her family's support, there isn't anyone who would have reason to try to take him."

"So we're left with no viable suspects," Beau summarized.

"If we're not looking for someone who was targeting a specific child, then we're looking for someone who likes little boys," Julian said dismally. It was the worst possibility because it guaranteed that there would be more victims, and the possibility that those next victims wouldn't be so lucky to just be drugged and left where they would be found was high.

"We're looking for a sexual predator," Abe said grimly, and no one disagreed with the sheriff.

"We need to check the sexual offenders' register. See if we have anyone within the vicinity who likes little boys," Beau said.

"I don't think he's going to be on the register," Julian said.

"Unfortunately, I agree with that," Abe said.

"He took the first two boys but didn't do anything with them besides drug them. He isn't confident enough yet to act out his fantasies. He takes them and probably thinks it will be easy to do whatever he wants with them, but when he actually goes to do it, he can't perform. The lack of confidence implies someone new at this. If they're new enough at it that they haven't been able to do anything yet then they're not on the list," Julian said.

"So, how are we going to find him?" Will asked.

"We didn't have any CCTV footage of any of the abductions," Fletcher said.

"And no witnesses besides the Miss Salsburys," Sydney added. "They didn't see much of anything, certainly not enough to help us."

"They remember a light-colored truck being the kidnapper's vehicle, none of our families own such a vehicle," Julian said, further proof that these abductions weren't committed by anyone related to one of the boys.

"A guy in a blue beanie driving a light-colored truck is not enough to narrow anything down," Will said.

"What's our next move?" Fletcher asked Abe.

Abe pondered this for a moment. "We need to go through any reports of a peeping Tom in River's End or any of the surrounding towns," Abe said. "And we need to go down to the school and any other places where the little boys hang out, sports clubs, scouts, the park, anything where someone might be watching them. We speak to teachers, coaches, see if they have seen anyone hanging around, specifically watching the boys. Then we'll need to speak with all the families in town who have boys under the age of thirteen and see if they've noticed anyone hanging around watching their sons. We should talk to the boys too, see if anyone has been contacting them on any social media sites, or anyone around town offering them candy or puppies or anything to draw them away from the pack and get them on their own."

It was a lot to do, would require them to speak with hundreds of people, all of that would take time, time they didn't have. This guy might be lacking in confidence, but he had gone after three boys in just a matter of days, and Rowan very well could have been the one he finally acted out his fantasies with.

River's End was a small town, the population was only around ten thousand people, but within that ten thousand were several hundred boys who fit the kidnapper's MO. That meant a lot of possible targets, too many for them to watch over, and even with precautions too many to make sure they all followed safety rules.

This guy was careful, he hadn't left any forensics behind, and he had been careful with the abductions, not leaving any witnesses behind, this last one excluded. Someone smart like that wasn't going to start laying low, and he wasn't going to hold off forever. Unless they could stop him sooner rather than later, he was going to follow through on the reason he'd taken the children.

# OCTOBER 8TH

11:19 A.M.

She shifted uncomfortably in her cramped position.

Mia felt like she had been here for hours, but in reality, it hadn't even quite been twenty minutes yet.

Most days, her team wasn't tasked with searching for someone who was lost or rescuing someone who was trapped or injured, so they spent a lot of their time running training scenarios. From water rescues to getting an injured person off the mountain, to searching for someone who had gotten lost, they tried to replicate scenarios that were as similar to those they would actually encounter, and they took turns at playing the lost or injured.

Today it was her turn.

So here she was, out in the forest on this particularly cold October morning, having left a trail of clues for her team to find as they searched for her. She had squirreled herself away behind some rocks and had to wait there for her team to find her. She had her radio on her, and if for some reason her team couldn't find her she would alert them to her hidey-hole, and then they would go back and debrief and figure out why they hadn't found her and what signs they had missed while tracking her so that it didn't happen again.

But Mia had faith in her team. They would find her. It wasn't a matter of if just of when, and as her legs were already cramping she hoped it was sooner rather than later.

Stretching her legs out, she reached down to grab hold of her toes and pulled them back, stretching out her cramped calf muscles. She had positioned herself close to the base. Sometimes there was the tendency to think that people got lost a long way from help, but sometimes they wandered close to help only they didn't know it was there and gave up. So she was less than a mile from the base camp building, and right about now she was wishing she was in out of the icy wind, her hands wrapped around a mug of steaming coffee instead of rubbing together to try to ward off the chill.

From where they had started off the search to the point where she was hiding was about four miles. If they covered a mile in a fifteen to twenty-minute window, then she probably had another hour or so to wait before they would find her.

Great.

Another hour out here in the cold, just what she needed.

And why was it so cold? It wasn't usually this chilly so early in October, and she suspected they were in for a cold winter. Last winter had been reasonably mild so it looked like this coming winter might want to make up for that.

Growing up in a small town, she and Julian had both spent most of their childhoods outdoors, and the cold didn't bother either one of them. When they were able to coordinate some time off, they had enjoyed exploring the beautiful part of the world they lived in. They both skied, they both owned snowmobiles, they both enjoyed hiking even if it was through the snow, and they'd spent a lot of happy days out here in the forest.

Maybe they could have more of those times again.

Things seemed to be looking promising. They were having dinner tonight, and she was determined that they would sit down and talk after dinner and hash out their issues. It was important to do that before either of them got anymore invested than they already were.

Who was she kidding? She was already invested.

At least one part of her life was looking up, but she'd been shocked when she saw her dad last night. It had been nearly three weeks since she'd last seen him, they'd both been busy, and they talked almost every day on the phone, so seeing him again had been heartbreaking. He'd lost weight, his normally twinkling blue eyes were sunken and dulled by pain, and he looked tired. His normally neat and tidy house had been untidy, and while it was nothing dramatic in terms of cleanliness, it was just that seeing it made her realize just how little energy he had left just to get through the normal day-to-day chores.

She had to convince him to come and stay with her, she knew it, she just didn't know how to make it happen.

"Stubborn man," she muttered.

Mia was just shifting again because her bottom felt like it was going numb sitting on the cold, hard rock when she heard the crunch of leaves and sticks that indicated someone was coming.

Was that her team already?

They'd certainly made good time.

She had specifically chosen this spot because she could peek around the rock and watch them as they came toward her without them immediately being able to spot her. She scanned the surrounding area, but she couldn't see anyone. Maybe what she'd heard was just a rabbit or a bird or something else moving through the quiet forest.

Then that feeling came back.

That someone is out there, and they're watching you feeling.

That first night, when she was looking for Devin Deville, she'd thought that it might be whoever had taken him still in the area and watching her. She'd thought the same thing when she was looking for Parker Barrett, but now she wasn't out here searching for a lost kid she was out here on a training exercise. There shouldn't be anyone else out there.

Just then a horrible thought occurred to her.

What if whoever was grabbing the little boys of River's End had a hideout here in the forest?

What if she was close to it?

It was too close to the base for someone to think they could get away with kidnapping little boys and keeping them, yet sometimes hiding in plain sight worked.

This spot was about halfway between where the two boys had been found, that would make it a good base for some pervert who was looking for a quiet location to set himself up. It didn't even have to be anything permanent, just a spot to set up a tent or something, or even right out in the open. They were fairly close to an access road, and even though the base was only a mile away it wasn't like she or her team were in this exact part of the forest every day.

Anxiety mounting, Mia looked around searching for any signs that someone had been using this area or something nearby. When she heard the sounds of footsteps, she ducked back down.

Someone was coming.

She was sure of it.

A small animal didn't make those sounds, and there were no large animals in this immediate vicinity which meant that it had to be a person.

Her breathing sounded inordinately loud, and she pressed a hand to her mouth in an attempt to stifle it. The footsteps were coming closer.

While she was hidden behind here if someone was looking for her they would find her, it was inevitable; depending on where they were standing and which direction they were facing they would notice her.

The footsteps were coming closer. Whoever it was had to be just a couple of yards away from her hiding space.

Then a shadow fell over her, and she scrunched her eyes closed as though that would make her disappear.

"Mia."

She shrieked when someone said her name. Actually shrieked at the sound of the voice and the presence above her.

"Are you okay?" Eileen asked, crouching down in front of her.

"Did you hurt yourself?"

"Eileen," she said on an exhale. Relief made her lightheaded for a moment, but she brushed it away and planted her hands on the rocks to lever herself up. The rest of her team were all there too, watching her with thinly veiled concern. "Sorry, no I'm fine, not hurt, I guess I just let my imagination run away with me."

"You've been under a lot of stress lately," Eileen tutted sympathetically. "Everything with your dad, and now this thing with Julian. Plus searching for two missing boys in less than a week was a stress none of us needed."

"Yeah, you're right I guess," she said as she stepped out from behind the rocks. Her friend had to be right. There hadn't been anyone out there when she was searching for the boys, and there wasn't anyone out there now, she had to get herself under control. She hadn't gone on a holiday in a while maybe that was what she needed, a break from everything where she could just rest and relax and find her equilibrium again.

"Course I'm right," Eileen said with a grin as she playfully nudged her shoulder.

Mia smiled back, albeit with less enthusiasm, and then snapped herself back into work mode. "Okay, guys, you made good time," she said as she started walking back toward the base. "I want a list of all the signs you saw that led you to me, I want to make sure that you didn't miss any. Were there any issues?" she asked, wondering if they had seen something that might make her feel like she wasn't balancing precariously on the ledge between sane and insane.

Was she really losing it?

She felt like she was, and she hadn't felt this way since the early days of her stalker's reign of terror. Back when she thought she was imagining that things in her house were moving, getting lost, disappearing, and then reappearing.

But that wasn't what was happening now.

Now she was just overworked and over-stressed.

A little time off was all she needed.

Maybe she and her dad could take a trip, spend as much time together as they could before he passed away.

Maybe Julian would come with them.

That brought a smile to her face, and she was able to set aside her worries and focus on her job.

\* \* \* \* \*

2:28 P.M.

"Beau, look," Julian said, pointing across the schoolyard to the trees on the other side.

"There's someone there," Beau said, following his gaze.

"Think it could be him?"

"Only one way to find out."

Pretending they were leaving the school, they headed to their car, parked in front of the school office. They got in and drove off in the opposite direction not wanting to alert their suspect that they were onto him until they were ready.

Their suspect was one Sebastian Welk. Thirty-two years old and new to River's End, he'd worked as the art teacher at the local elementary school up until about a month ago when he had been let go after an incident involving a couple of the boys. Sebastian had taken a group of third and fourth graders and had them participate in a photography session. While none of the photos were sexually explicit, some of them had been deemed to be inappropriate, and the man had lost his job.

Apparently, that hadn't been the end of him though. Sebastian had continued to come around the school, hanging around just outside the property—according to the principal, he *never* stepped foot on school property—and watching the kids playing.

All the children who had been involved in the photoshoot were boys and between the ages of eight and ten, just like their three victims.

Sebastian Welk was their best suspect at the moment, and they needed to talk to the man and see what he had to say for himself. There was no criminal record, but they had expected the man they were looking for was just starting out, which was why he lacked in confidence.

Beau drove the car around and parked it about half a mile from where they had seen a man standing watching the kids in the playground. They started walking toward the school, and Julian stopped.

"Look," he said quietly, gesturing to what had caught his attention.

"A car," Beau said.

"A light gray truck," he added. "Just like the one that was seen driving away from Rowan's near abduction."

As they walked over to the vehicle, Julian ran the license plate and a moment later received confirmation that the truck belonged to Sebastian.

"He's coming," Beau said softly.

They both moved off, one on either side of the vehicle, both hidden behind trees as they waited for Sebastian to show himself.

A moment later, Julian saw him walking this way. With a nod at Beau, they stepped out of their hiding places with guns drawn. They both knew what desperate people were capable of.

"Sebastian Welk, I'm Deputy Black. Please put your hands on your head and get down on your knees," he instructed as he pointed his gun at the man.

Eyes growing wide, Sebastian's gaze bounced between him and Beau before he abruptly spun around and ran off.

"I hate when they run." Julian sighed as he took off after the man, Beau on his heels.

Sebastian was overweight and out of shape, and it didn't take long for him and Beau to catch up. Throwing himself at Sebastian, he tackled the other man to the ground and easily restrained him, snapping a pair of handcuffs onto his wrists and securing them behind his back.

Together he and Beau dragged Sebastian up onto his feet to find that the other man was crying quietly. As far as he was concerned, that was as good as an admission of guilt.

"Why did you run, Mr. Welk?" he asked as they walked him back toward their car.

"I … I … you're the … I didn't think … I'm sorry," the man stammered desperately. He made no further move to try to escape, but still Julian made sure he kept a firm hand on the man's arm.

"Yeah, you didn't think," he agreed. "You know why we're here?"

"They were just photos," Sebastian said immediately. "The boys weren't naked or anything, it wasn't anything sexual. I just thought it would be fun for them to take some photos in the river, you know because the town is called River's End."

"You find wet little boys arousing, Mr. Welk?" Beau asked with barely concealed disgust.

"N-no," Sebastian said, but it wasn't very convincing.

"Did you have copies of those photos on your personal computer?" Julian asked. They already knew that he had, the principal had filled them in on all the details, but he wanted to see if Sebastian was going to lie or not.

"Well, yes, but no, I mean the laptop was from the school. I used it for work and took it home with me. I don't have another computer," Sebastian explained anxiously.

"So I'll take that as a yes," he said. "You had those photos of those kids at your home."

"Was Devin Deville one of those boys who took part in your play in the river photoshoot?" Beau asked. "What about Parker Barrett? Rowan Douglas?"

"I, um, well, I think, yes, I mean, I think they were. Devin is in the fourth grade, and Parker and Rowan in the third grade, so yes,

I think they probably, I mean I suppose they would be, but um, I would have to check to confirm," Sebastian stammered.

Pouncing on that admission, Julian asked, "So you still have copies of all of those photos even though you lost your job and your laptop was confiscated?"

Sebastian almost tripped over his own feet as he realized he had made a crucial mistake. "Umm …" he trailed off and didn't offer them anymore.

"I thought you said you didn't have another computer," Beau said.

"I don't," Sebastian agreed quickly.

"You got them on your phone?" Julian asked, assuming the bulge in Sebastian's back pocket was his cell.

"N-no, I well, we were going to, I mean the point of the project was to take the photos and make our own river using paint and crafts and things and then print out the pictures and add them to our river. Some of the photos were already printed when I was fired."

"And you just had to take them with you?" Beau demanded.

"Well, um …" Sebastian looked to him like he was going to provide assistance, but when the man saw Julian's hard face he started to cry again. "They were just pictures, I mean I kind of liked looking at them, but I wouldn't hurt a real kid. I swear I wouldn't."

"You know you just admitted to using the photos as child pornography," Beau said harshly.

"I … I mean … I didn't … they were just photos," Sebastian said again.

"They *were*," Julian agreed. "Until they weren't enough. They couldn't get you off anymore, you needed more, you needed the real thing. Is that what you were going to do with them, put them in the river while you watched and touched yourself? You were a science teacher before you moved here, weren't you, Mr. Welk?"

"Y-yes."

"So you would know how to make your own Rohypnol if you had to, wouldn't you?"

"I ... I ... you would need a lab to ... to do that."

"That's not a denial," Beau noted.

"You drugged the kids because you didn't want them to be scared. You wanted to be able to use them to get what you needed without the hassle of dealing with a terrified child. But when it was time to actually make your fantasy a reality you backed out, couldn't go through with it. You didn't want Devin to be hurt though so you left him where you knew he would be found. You did the same for Parker. Were you gaining confidence each time? Was Rowan going to be the one? How long, Mr. Welk, how long until you were ready to start touching them, hurting them?"

"I didn't, I wouldn't," Sebastian balked at the accusation.

"But you would," he contradicted. "You couldn't help yourself. You had to touch them, you had to take from them what you needed. You would have touched them. You would have hurt them. It was only a matter of time."

"No," Sebastian wept. "You're wrong, no, no. I love boys, I would never hurt them, I wouldn't."

They all knew it was a lie.

Sebastian Welk was a sexual predator, a pedophile. Sooner or later he would have followed through and started acting out his fantasies. Julian would bet anything that Devin, Parker, and Rowan's photos were amongst the ones he had printed before he was found out. The ones he had no doubt masturbated to as he dreamed about what it would feel like to make his fantasies a reality.

Thankfully, Sebastian was now in custody. When they searched his house he was sure they would find the photos, and that combined with the fact that Sebastian had taken them out to the river would be enough to press charges. Julian was sure that wherever Sebastian had taken those photos was close to where the boys had been found in the forest. That spot factored into the fantasy.

If they were lucky, this case would be closed by the end of the day, and he wouldn't have to worry about any more little boys being kidnapped, which would leave him free and clear to focus on Mia.

* * * * *

6:24 P.M.

A glance at the clock on the wall in her living room told her there were still six minutes to go until Julian would be here to pick her up. Although if she knew him then he would probably be here any minute now, the military had definitely drilled into him the need to be on time or early.

Mia smoothed a hand down her simple black knee-length skirt, which she'd paired with black ankle boots and her favorite purple sweater. It was a pretty shade of lavender with a cable pattern, and wearing it helped give her a little confidence, which she felt severely lacking in.

Dating again was weird, especially with someone she had been with since she was a kid, that she was technically still married to, and although she was determined to give this a real go, she still had reservations that they could fix the problems that had led to their break up in the first place.

The doorbell rang with four minutes to go, and Mia drew in a last steadying breath before opening the door and quickly finding all the air sucked out of her lungs.

Julian stood there dressed in a pair of black pants and a white button-down shirt, looking ridiculously sexy. If it were possible, he'd bulked up in muscle even more since they'd broken up and she maybe drooled a little thinking about what those muscles were going to feel like when she got him naked later.

Huh.

She hadn't been sure that tonight was going to end with anything more than a kiss on the doorstep, but apparently her subconscious mind had other plans.

"You look gorgeous," Julian said, giving her an appreciative once over and Mia felt herself blush. It had been a long time since she had felt beautiful, but the way Julian was looking at her made her feel like the prettiest woman in the world.

"So do you," she said and couldn't not step closer, place her hands on his biceps, and stand on tiptoes to kiss him.

Immediately he dragged her closer and deepened the kiss until the whole world faded away and all that existed were her and Julian and his lips on hers making her body come alive in a way she had feared it never would again.

"Mia-bug," he said on a moan. "I would love to carry you upstairs and spend the night worshiping your body, but we have to go to dinner."

Somewhat reluctantly, she released her hold on him and stepped back only to be hauled forward again so she was tucked against Julian's side with his arm wrapped around her waist.

"Got everything you need?" he asked as he snagged her purse from the table by the door.

"Yep. So where are we going?" she asked as they walked down to where his car was parked on the street in front of her house.

"You'll see when we get there." Julian opened her door for her and waited for her to get in before crossing around to the driver's side. "What?"

"Trying to figure out why you're acting all secretive. This is River's End not New York City, it's not like there are that many places to go to get a meal. We can go to the diner, the Honeysuckle Hotel, the bakery if we're going to be done by seven, or the ice cream parlor if all you want is dessert."

Julian just grinned. "You used to love surprises."

"I used to love a lot of things," she muttered. It was true, she had always loved surprises, never been the kid who snooped through the house looking for hidden Christmas present, or the girlfriend who hounded about what he had planned for dates or special occasions, but being stalked had kind of taken all the fun out of being surprised. It was safe to say she had had enough surprises to last a lifetime.

"I know, babe, but this is a good surprise. Let go of all the anxiety and just relax. You know you're safe here," he reminded her, reaching over to lay a hand on her thigh.

He was right, and she allowed his words to break through the tension building inside her and threatening to ruin the night, and instead relaxed and curled her fingers around Julian's hand. He turned their hands over so hers was on the bottom, his thumb brushing softly across the inside of her wrist, a place he knew she was particularly sensitive, and her whole body began to unravel until she felt like a puddle of goo.

All of a sudden, she realized that they had left the town behind them and were now out in the forest. "Where are we going?" she asked again, intrigued now. She had just assumed they would be having dinner somewhere in town, but it looked like Julian had decided to be a little more inventive.

"Right here," he said as he turned the car off the main road, navigating it between a few trees then stopping about fifty yards away from the road.

"Here?" she echoed, looking around and trying to figure out where exactly they were.

Then she saw it.

The treehouse.

She and a bunch of the other kids had spent a whole summer building it. It was huge and like a real little house up in the branches of a large fir tree. She had forgotten all about this place, but back in the day, it had been the center of their lives. They would come out here after school, and on weekends, they'd play games and have sleepovers, and as they got older it was make out central.

Julian opened her door for her, and she launched herself at him, hugging him hard. He lifted her feet off the ground and held her just as tightly.

"This was where we shared our first kiss," he whispered in her ear.

Mia remembered that night well. They'd been thirteen, it was the middle of summer, they were out late because it was summer vacation and they didn't have school the next day. They had spent the day with the other kids, swimming in the river, swinging on the rope swing into the water, and dunking each other, then they'd built a fire in the fire pit and sat around laughing and talking. Julian had taken her hand and led her up into the treehouse under the guise of getting more snacks. As soon as they were alone, he'd taken her face between his hands and leaned in and kissed her. At first she'd been surprised, but then she'd melted into it and loved every second of that awkward adolescent kiss.

"I remember," she said breathily.

"I thought it was the perfect spot to start over." He set her on her feet, then led her over to the old fire pit which she now saw had a fire crackling away in it. Beside the fire pit, there was a picnic blanket spread out on the ground, Sitting on it was a thermos, a plate or Pop-Tarts covered in cling wrap, a covered bowl of popcorn, and two bottles of soda.

Mia couldn't help but laugh. "This is what you used to make for me when we were thirteen, and you didn't know how to cook."

"I thought it would be fun to pretend we were thirteen again and everything was easy." The look on his face said he was having second thoughts about that plan and wondering if maybe she would have preferred a fancy dinner with candles and flowers, but this was perfect.

Reaching up to kiss his cheek, she whispered in his ear, "I

hope we get to do a little more than kiss awkwardly like we did when we were thirteen." Yep, her body definitely had hot and heavy plans for the end of this date.

Julian's body rumbled with a deep laugh. "Oh, yeah, we can do more than kiss like we're still thirteen."

As he guided her to the blanket and she sat down, Julian beside her, she realized that this wasn't just any old picnic blanket. This was the exact same one that Julian used to sneak out of his aunt's house so they would have something to sit on when they used to come out here for secret dates after everyone else had gone to bed.

Had he kept this?

Her eyes flew to his, silently seeking an answer.

He smiled at her, tucking a lock of hair behind her ear then letting his fingers caress her cheek. "I couldn't throw it away. I know it's silly and ridiculously sentimental, but I took this with me when I was deployed. I would pull it out sometimes when I was feeling homesick and missing you. It reminded me of all the good times we had shared together. It made me feel closer to you."

Tears blurred her vision. That was perhaps the sweetest thing she had ever heard in her life.

Scrambling onto his lap, Mia wrapped her arms around his neck and kissed him.

\* \* \* \* \*

6:40 P.M.

Mia's tears dripped down onto his cheeks, but from the way she was kissing him, Julian knew that they were happy tears.

He was so glad he had brought her out here, back to where it all began, where they had shared their first kiss, spent their first real date, and then so many other happy hours. They used to sit out here in the middle of the night and talk for hours, telling each other all their secrets.

In fact, Mia was the only person on the planet who knew all of his.

His love for her was all-consuming, and now that he had her sitting on his lap kissing him like she needed him to live, he couldn't quite remember the reason why he had left or why he stayed away for so long.

Before he could pass the point of no return, Julian gently eased her back, this wasn't where they had made love for the first time. Mia had deserved better than sex on a picnic blanket in the middle of the forest then, and she deserved better now. When they made love again it would be in a bed where he could take his time and worship every inch of her.

Mia's green eyes were glittery with desire in the light of the fire, and Julian very nearly gave in to the need that was pulsing through his body with each beat of his heart. This woman amazed him, what she had survived, what she had overcome, how she had thrived and grown stronger, that she hadn't lost her ability to love and care about others. She had every reason to have given up and let the darkness claim her, but she hadn't.

"My sweet, Mia-bug." He took her face in his hands and let his fingertips trace across her soft skin as he drank in the sight of her and the feel of her and the knowledge that she could be his again. "Baby, I missed you so much."

"I know, I missed you too." She leaned forward and rested her forehead on his. "When you were deployed, I used to come out here some nights when I couldn't sleep," she admitted. "I would sit up in the treehouse or I would sit here by the fire pit, or sometimes I would go skinny dipping just like we used to when we were teenagers."

"Mia," he groaned. Picturing her naked in the river was not helping him with his plan to wait until they could make love in a bed before doing more than kiss her.

She laughed before sobering. "After you left, sometimes I

would come out here to remember better times."

"I did too," he told her.

"You did?" she sounded surprised.

"This was our place, Mia. I know the other kids hung out here too, but this place was our special place, and when it felt like my chest couldn't expand from the weight of missing you crushing it, I would come out here so I could breathe again."

She smiled at him, that winning smile that lit up her whole face, a smile he had been so afraid he would never see on her face again. "It's a wonder we didn't end up here at the same time."

From the way she said it, it was clear she wondered if they had both been there at the same time if it would have changed anything, leading them back to each other sooner. He was wondering the same thing. "I have a confession to make," he told her, deciding that if they were starting over, they were doing so with a clean slate.

Mia arched one brow and waited.

"I saw you here one night last summer," he admitted. "You were in the river, water streaming off you, standing there in the moonlight like a goddess."

"If you saw me, why didn't you say something?" Mia cocked her head to the side, obviously puzzled.

"I wanted to—so badly—but you were crying, and ..." he trailed off, unable to put into words how deeply her tears had affected him.

"I cried, Julian. I cried a lot after you left, but that night that you're talking about those were happy tears. They were tears of letting go, of not allowing what Joshua did to me to control the rest of my life. That night I felt free, that's why I went in the water. Usually, I would just sit here and think, but that night I felt like I was being reborn like I was starting over, like the past was being washed away."

He should have gone to her then and saved them both several months more of the agony of being apart.

Should haves couldn't be changed, but he could do something about it now.

"You looked so beautiful," he murmured, letting his fingers run through her silky locks which hung loosely around her shoulders. "When I saw you all I wanted was to touch you."

"You're touching me now," she whispered in a sultry voice.

"Not enough," he whispered back.

Her green eyes met his, and he saw a reflection of his own need. "Kiss me, Julian."

Not needing to be told twice, he claimed her lips as his hands moved to span her waist. Her arms were curled around his shoulders lifting the hem of her sweater enough that he got a glimpse of soft white skin. He couldn't look and not touch, and his fingers trailed across her stomach, working their way slowly higher.

When he brushed against the underside of Mia's breasts, she sucked in a breath, then moaned into his mouth as he took her breasts into his hands. Her nipples went hard, and he teased them through the thin, silky material of her bra.

Mia wriggled against him, and that immediately had him growing hard. The plan to wait until they were in a bed seemed to be slipping away. He wanted her, and from the way she was kissing him and squirming in his lap, Mia wanted him too.

With nimble fingers, he unsnapped her bra, groaning as her small round breasts came free and one fell into his hand. Like he was some adolescent kid who couldn't control his hormones, he almost came in his pants from the simple act of touching the woman he loved and her little panting breaths. As he rolled one of her nipples between his thumb and forefinger Mia began to move restlessly.

"More," she said breathily.

Happy to oblige, he took hold of the hem of her sweater and pulled it over her head, tossing it to the side along with her bra. Not to be left on the sidelines, as he kissed her and fondled her breasts, Mia began unbuttoning his shirt with an almost frenetic energy, and he knew both of them had been thinking about this for a long time.

"Boots off, skirt too, I want you naked and in the river," he whispered in her ear as he kissed the side of her neck.

Mia shivered, but from the glazed look in her eyes, he knew she was going to agree before she nodded and scrambled to her feet to remove her ankle boots and skirt. She stood before him, a blonde goddess, wearing nothing but a pair of purple satin panties and a sexy smile.

She was almost too perfect to be true.

But she was true, and she was his.

He shoved off his shirt, removed his shoes, pants, and boxers, then took the hand Mia held out and pulled her to him. She came willingly—eagerly—and he lifted her off her feet and into his arms. Mia wrapped her legs around his waist, her hot, wet center tempting him, but he wasn't ready yet, he needed to make sure Mia came before he even considered his own release.

Carrying her toward the water he knew was going to be cold, he alternated between kissing her and drawing her nipples into his mouth and suckling, drawing moan after moan from Mia as her fingers tangled in his hair, and her head fell back as pleasure began to assault her.

Julian sucked in a breath as he stepped into the water, Mia did the same, but she quickly recovered and urged his mouth back to her breast.

Keeping one arm locked underneath her bottom, his other hand zeroed in on her heat. Pushing aside the thin material of her panties, he slipped a finger inside her, his thumb finding her little bundle of nerves, working both simultaneously.

Never one to sit back and take without giving anything in return, Mia reached down and took him in her hand, and while he stroked deep inside her and pressed harder on her nub, she increased the pace as she ran her hand up and down his hard length.

Like they were one person they both hit their peak simultaneously, crying out their pleasure into each other's mouths.

\* \* \* \* \*

7:12 P.M.

What had they done?

That had been amazing, incredible, better than she had remembered, but they hadn't talked through their issues yet so they shouldn't be standing in the river, naked, having just made out.

As though sensing the change in her demeanor, Julian set her on her feet, already emotionally withdrawing from her.

"Sorry, we shouldn't have done that," he said.

"I wanted to," she assured him.

He cocked his head, studied her as though he didn't believe her. "You don't regret what we just did?"

Her hesitation was enough to have him turning his back on her and walking toward the shore. "No, Julian, wait." His legs were longer than hers and could make it through the water quicker than she could, and by the time she reached him, he was already at the picnic blanket throwing his clothes back on. "Would you stop and listen for a moment."

He complied, but when he turned around his face was a blank mask.

This wasn't what she wanted.

How had things gone from amazing to awful in the space of a minute?

"I don't regret what we did, not at all. I just made a promise to myself that we weren't going to do … that …" she gestured to the river behind them, "until we had talked. When you packed up your things and left it just about broke me." She held up a hand when pain washed away the emptiness on his face, and he opened his mouth to no doubt apologize. "No, I'm not angry with you for leaving, I know why you did. We were at an impasse, and your leaving was the shove I needed to start dealing with what happened. But just because I understand, doesn't mean it didn't hurt or that I'm not scared of getting hurt again. Julian, we have so much to talk through, so many issues to address, and I don't want to get my hopes up only to find that the same issues that drove us apart will keep us apart."

His face softened, and he took a step closer, reaching out to gently cup her cheek in his hand. "Too late, sweetheart. My hopes are already up, and I think yours are too."

She shivered as much at his touch as his words.

He was right.

Her hopes were already soaring.

"But you're right, we do need to talk, and we should do that before we go any further. So how about we put our clothes back on, sit down, eat our dinner of pop tarts and ramen noodles and talk."

No sooner were the words out of his mouth than both of their phones began to ring. "That can't be good," Mia said as she located her purse and dug around in it for her cell phone. By the time she found it and pressed accept, Julian was already talking to whoever had called him. "Hello?"

"Mia, it's Lyle. We have another missing kid."

She thought they were done with this. Poppy had told her that they had a man in custody who was suspected as being the abductor of the three little boys, so who was missing and why? "Who is it?"

"Tammy Martins."

Her forehead creased in confusion. Tammy Martins was an eleven-year-old girl who had only just recently moved with her family to River's End. "What happened? How did she go missing?"

"Walking home from a friend's house, she never made it. Her school bag and shoes were found by the road a few miles south of where the boys' things were found."

"Do we think this is the same person?"

"Circumstances are similar."

Unfortunately, Lyle was right. "I'll be there in less than fifteen minutes."

By the time she hung up and looked over at Julian, he was already fully dressed and holding out her bra, which she took and quickly pulled on.

"I'm guessing your phone call was the same as mine," she said as she picked up her skirt.

"Tammy Martins is missing," Julian said.

"Three boys and now a girl, that doesn't make any sense," she said, frustrated as she pulled her sweater over her head. "Pedophiles don't usually go after both boys and girls. Especially when he had a clearly defined victim type. And besides, I thought you had the guy."

"We thought we did," Julian told her as he packed up the picnic dinner they weren't going to get to enjoy. "Either we were wrong or this isn't related to the other cases."

"Hard to believe it isn't. Another child going missing in the same circumstances as the others." Bag on her shoulder she headed toward Julian's car.

"Ah, Mia, I think you forgot something."

When she turned around she saw Julian holding her boots, a grin on his face.

"Right," she said with a laugh. "I guess I'm a little eager to get going."

"Agreed, but you won't get far without shoes," Julian teased.

The next hour was a flurry of activity. They drove out to the search and rescue base, she changed into appropriate clothing— pleased she always kept several spare changes of clothes in her locker—then briefed her team, and they divided up search areas.

Then they all headed out.

The evening was clear, the sky bright with starlight and moonlight, a lot of which managed to filter through the trees and light her way. This definitely wasn't how she had expected the night to turn out. She'd expected dinner in a restaurant, then talking through their issues, followed by making love. Instead, she'd gotten dinner at the river which they hadn't had time to eat, making out in the water, and a search for a missing child. She was definitely disappointed that they'd been interrupted because they needed to talk, she wanted those little niggling doubts that nothing had changed to go away so she could focus on the future, but her job was important, search and rescue often came down to a matter of hours between life and death.

Suddenly, a sense of déjà vu settled heavily over her.

It wasn't just that she was out here for the fourth time this week looking for a missing kid, it was that feeling of being watched. Every time she was out in the forest alone she felt it, and she was starting to believe that it wasn't just her imagination running away from her.

Someone else was out there.

She was sure of it. Eyes were following her every move from someone who knew how to move silently and not leave a trail.

The kidnapper?

Since another child had been kidnapped, it was reasonable to assume that whoever had been arrested wasn't the man they were looking for which meant the real kidnapper was still out there.

What did he want with the children?

Why did he abduct them but then leave them unharmed and where they were sure to be found?

What game was he playing?

It felt like something else was going on here, but she had no idea what. She was a search and rescue worker, not a cop, she didn't deal with criminals just with people who were unlucky enough to get hurt out in rough terrain or lost.

Something snapped close by, and she froze.

"Hello?" she called out, willing her voice to come out calm and confident and not betray the near terror that was swirling inside her.

Nobody answered.

"Tammy, is that you? Call out if you're nearby, honey. This is Mia from search and rescue. We're going to find you, okay?"

No reply.

"Tammy? Can you hear me?"

Nothing.

"Is someone else out there? If you're hurt or lost then I'm here to help. If you tell me where you are I'll get you out of here."

She stood and waited, but all she could hear was her own breathing and the echo of her pulse drumming in her ears.

If someone was out here, they could probably sneak right up behind her, and despite her training, she wouldn't even hear them coming.

What was wrong with her?

As soon as she got out here she felt like she was losing her mind. She would have sworn till she was blue in the face that she wasn't alone and someone kept watching her while she was on searches, but as soon as she was back in the town going about the rest of her life she felt completely normal.

Shaking off the feeling of impending dread, Mia kept walking, calling out every so often for Tammy but never getting an answer.

She had been walking for maybe another five minutes when she heard it.

Footsteps.

No longer disguised, they were coming right for her.

Deciding to trust her gut and assume that something wasn't right, Mia was pulling her radio out when a figure dressed all in black rushed her.

She tried to spin out of the way, but her maneuver was cut off when the person attacked with more ferocity than she had been expecting.

Something slammed into her head, dropping her immediately to the ground, the radio falling from her hand.

She tried to reach for it, but her attacker stomped on it, shattering the device and any hope she had of calling for help.

Mia tried to get up, knowing that she had to fight back if she stood a chance at surviving this, but her body wouldn't cooperate, and the pain in her head grew too strong, plunging her into unconsciousness.

\* \* \* \* \*

8:52 P.M.

Julian scanned the small crowd, but he didn't see her.

That first little tingling of concern that told him something wasn't right started in his gut and only grew when he did a more careful look around and still didn't see Mia.

She should be here.

He'd found Tammy Martins within the first ten minutes of his search. She had been close to the base, almost like someone wanted the search team to stumble upon her quickly.

Why?

There had to be a reason.

And why did their kidnapper switch from boys to girls? Most pedophiles had a type, and all three previous victims had been young boys between the ages of eight and ten. Then all of a sudden their guy was grabbing an eleven-year-old girl. It didn't make sense, unless …

They'd warned all families with young boys as well as the kids themselves not to be out alone for any reason. Stick in groups, stay close to adults, no walking to and from school, friends' houses, the park, or anywhere on your own. They had effectively wiped out the kidnapper's target group which meant he had to switch things up if he wanted to keep doing what he was doing. That the kidnapper had done so, so easily implied that the who didn't matter, he would take whoever was an easy mark.

The only reason to do that would be if the boys were part of a bigger picture. A picture they had yet to figure out or even notice.

"Lyle?" he called out, heading straight for the older man. "Have you seen Mia?"

"No." Lyle looked around as though needing to confirm that. "The call went out that Tammy had been found and for all searchers to head back to base. She should be here."

"She should," he agreed.

"You think something's happened to her? I don't think there's anyone more surefooted than Mia, but accidents can still happen, and the only way she wouldn't call in was if she couldn't."

"I don't think she fell," he murmured, that feeling in his gut that something was wrong, that Mia was in danger, was growing.

Lyle's eyes widened. "You think someone got to her? The kidnapper?"

"Missing kids turning up unharmed, just drugged so they were easy to deal with, a supposed pedophile that switched from boys to girls without missing a beat? Something here isn't adding up. I'm going out to look for her."

"I'll round up everyone and send them out too," Lyle said.

Julian nodded. "And call for another ambulance." Unfortunately, he agreed with Lyle's assessment that the only reason Mia wouldn't call in or return was because she couldn't.

Not bothering to wait for Lyle to spread the word and send the team back out, Julian headed off into the forest, making his way toward what had been Mia's search area.

The more he walked, the more his concerns grew. Mia had been the one who had found all three of the missing boys. Had she seen something? Someone? No, she would have put it in her reports if she had seen anyone out there who shouldn't have been. But that didn't mean that they hadn't seen her.

Had she become a liability?

If the kidnapper believed that she had seen him or something that could point to him, then he might have decided that she needed to be taken out. Sebastian Welk was obviously not their kidnapper. However, he would be charged with possession of child pornography. Those photos from the river had some of the boys without their tops on which would qualify it as porn. Grabbing Tammy could have been a way to get Mia out here and alone so the kidnapper could get to her. It would explain why the kidnapper was able to so easily go after a girl.

Julian froze when he heard the sound of a car engine.

Someone else was out here and with a vehicle.

While you could off-road through the forest, there was no road and no reason why anyone else should be out here.

If you needed to dispose of a body or transport someone somewhere, then you would need a car.

When he spotted headlights up ahead, Julian pulled out his gun—thankful he never went anywhere without it—and started running.

The car was stopped, and he could make out a shadowy figure getting out of the driver's door.

"Hey," he yelled out. "Police, stay right there where I can see you."

Whoever it was chose not to obey his orders and flung themselves back inside the vehicle, revving the engine and taking off.

Aiming, he fired off a shot, connecting with one of the back tires as the vehicle swerved between trees, but it wasn't enough to render the truck undrivable. There was no point in trying to go after it on foot, blown-out tire or not, the vehicle could make better time than he could.

Instead, he ran toward the small lump lying on the ground.

Mia.

Skidding to his knees at her side, he immediately curled a hand under her jaw and touched his fingertips to her neck.

Relief knocked him onto his backside when he found a pulse.

"Mia, honey, can you hear me?" As carefully as he could, Julian rolled Mia over so she was lying on her back, his gaze immediately zeroing in on the blood streaking her face and a lump the size of an egg on her temple. In the light of the moon, her blood glowed black and stood out in stark contrast to her pasty white complexion.

She didn't answer his question, nor did she stir when he moved her, she was out cold.

"Lyle, it's Julian," he said into his radio. "I found Mia, she's unconscious. Someone hit her over the head and was going to put her into a vehicle when I arrived."

"What?" the man sputtered. "Someone tried to abduct her?"

"I'm guessing she saw something she shouldn't. Whoever it was took off when I arrived, I shot out a back tire, but they were still able to drive away. I'm going to carry her back. Given someone tried to kidnap her I don't want to wait around for a team to get here, I want her someplace safe as soon as possible."

"Ambulance is on the way," Lyle said, his voice tight with restrained anger.

Julian knew the feeling.

Mia had been through enough, more than enough, more than anyone should ever have to, and now someone wanted to hurt her—abduct her—just because she'd seen something she didn't even know she'd seen.

Unacceptable.

Putting away his radio, he very gently scooped Mia up and into his arms. "I got you, baby," he whispered, lowering his head so he could touch a feather-light kiss to a spot on her forehead that wasn't covered in blood.

He knew that head injuries bled a lot, he'd had them, and he'd seen them on fellow soldiers, but seeing Mia covered in blood, so still in his arms, terrified him on a level he had only faced twice before. Once, when he witnessed his mother's death, and once when Mia's stalker had abducted her.

But Mia wasn't gone, and while she was still out her pulse was strong, and he had to believe that she would be okay.

"Still, it would make me feel a whole lot better if you opened those pretty green eyes for me, Mia-bug," he said as he carried her through the forest.

She didn't respond, but he could feel warm air against his neck and repeated on a loop through his mind that she was alive.

Alive was what mattered.

Injuries could be treated, dealt with, but dead rang with a finality that scared them all on some level.

"Come on, Mia-bug, you know I don't like begging. If you don't wake up soon I'm going to keep calling you Mia-bug, and I know how much you hate it."

Despite his worry, he couldn't not smile at the memory. They'd been fourteen, camping one hot summer night out in the forest at the treehouse along with a bunch of their friends. They'd talked till late around the campfire before finally they'd all climbed into their sleeping bags and gone to sleep.

Sometime later they had all been woken by the sounds of Mia's hysterical screams and frantic rolling about as she tried—unsuccessfully—to get out of her sleeping bag.

She'd placed it over an ant nest, and during the night the tiny insects had made their way inside her sleeping bag. She had a slight phobia when it came to bugs, and she'd completely freaked out.

Once they'd gotten her out and figured out what had happened, the other kids had laughed and teased her with the snug as a bug in a rug saying. Of course the teasing hadn't stopped with just that night, and within the month the nickname Mia-bug had stuck.

She'd hated it ever since.

That meant that he had of course started using it to needle her, but over time the nickname—for him at least—had turned into a term of endearment. She was his Mia-bug, and he loved having her snug in his embrace.

"Please, Mia," he begged.

A beat passed, and then a very weak, very groggy, and pain-filled voice whispered, "Julian?"

Just like that the world was righted again.

# OCTOBER 9TH

1:23 A.M.

"Hey, sweetheart, we're here."

The words hovered around her, hanging in the air, but she was tired, and she hurt, and she didn't want to wake up and figure out what was going on.

"Come on, honey, wake up for me, just for a moment then we'll get you all tucked into bed."

Bed sounded good, so Mia forced her eyes to open to find Julian crouched in the open car door. "I'm awake," she said softly. "Maybe you could help me inside before you go home?"

"Mia-bug, if you think I'm leaving you alone tonight then you hit your head harder than I thought and I'm taking you straight back to the hospital," he said, a disapproving frown on his face.

She chuckled then winced as it made pain slice through her head. "If you want I can call my dad."

"I don't want," he said simply. Then he reached inside and unclipped her seatbelt and gathered her into his arms.

Mia thought about telling him she could walk on her own, but her head pounded, and she was still a little dizzy, and anyway, she was right where she wanted to be. Julian hadn't left her side since she had woken up while he was carrying her back to search and rescue's base. He'd ridden with her in the ambulance, stayed with her while she was checked out in the ER, waited while she had a CT scan, then driven her back to her place once she was discharged. She was so grateful for his presence and the comfort it provided, but she was a big girl, and if he changed his mind and decided he wanted to head home she would be all right on her own.

Inside, he flicked on the lights and headed straight for her bedroom. "You take some painkillers and drink a little water and then straight off to sleep for you," he ordered.

She couldn't help but smile at his bossy tone. "I'm too tired to argue."

In the bedroom, he set her on her feet, keeping an arm around her waist so she didn't wobble and fall, while he pulled back the covers, then picked her up again and set her on the mattress, tucking her in. Sydney had stopped by her place earlier to grab her some pajamas to wear back from the hospital so she didn't have to change, she could just relax and go to sleep.

"I'll grab you some painkillers, try not to sleep until I get back," Julian said.

"I'll try," she murmured to his retreating back.

It couldn't have taken him more than two minutes to retrieve pills and a glass of water, but Mia was already dozing off by the time he returned.

All her strength seemed to have been sapped, and Julian had to slip an arm behind her shoulders and lift her and support her as she swallowed the painkillers and half the glass of water.

When he lowered her back down, his palm rested against her cheek, and his fingertips brushed lightly around the row of stitches Levi had put in to close the gash on her temple. She hadn't looked at it herself yet, but she was sure her face was going to be black and blue by morning if it wasn't already, and she'd be lucky if swelling didn't have her eye close. Still, she was alive, and she hadn't been abducted so that was a plus.

"Your touch takes away the pain better than any pills could," she said sleepily. She'd slept most of the evening, but she was still so tired.

"I'm glad. Now rest, sweetheart. I'll be sleeping in the chair if you need me."

She wanted to ask him to sleep in the bed with her, but she was the one who had made a big deal about not doing anything until they had talked, and his presence in the room would be enough for her to relax and rest.

Julian stooped, kissed her forehead, then hesitated a moment before kissing her lips. Then he fussed with the blankets, switched on the lamp on her nightstand, and settled into the rocking chair by the window.

Exhaustion took hold of her and she drifted away.

The next thing Mia knew sunlight was streaming in around her pink curtains, and a glance at the clock on the nightstand said it was after ten in the morning. Her headache had dulled a little but wouldn't be disappearing anytime soon.

She looked around the room, but there was no sign of Julian, and she saw a piece of white paper sitting on the chair he had spent the night in.

With a grimace, Mia managed to swing her legs over the side of the bed and slowly sit up. The wave of dizziness that hit her wasn't as bad as she had been expecting, and thankful for small mercies, she continued moving until she was standing.

When she didn't fall straight back down onto her bottom, Mia walked the four steps to the rocking chair on slightly wobbly legs and sank down into it while she read his note.

Good morning, my sweet Mia-bug,

I woke you up and kissed you goodbye before I had to leave for work, but you looked so groggy and sleepy I'm not sure you'll remember when you wake up.

I'll call to check in on you every few hours and make sure you CALL SOMEONE if you feel worse.

Love you

Julian

She rolled her eyes at the way he had used capital letters for the call someone part, knowing that she could be a little stubborn and that she wouldn't want to worry anyone. Despite that, she couldn't not smile. It was nice not to be alone anymore, to have someone to worry over her. Her dad worried about her of course, and her friends, but it was different having a partner to worry about you.

Deciding she may as well get on with her day, Mia stood and headed for her closet to grab some clothes and take a shower. She'd have to be careful not to get the stitches wet, but she could wash the rest of herself, and maybe tonight Julian would help her carefully wash her hair.

As she stripped off her pajamas and tossed them onto the bed, she turned the shower on as hot as it would go and examined herself in the mirror while she waited for the water to heat up. She had a pretty spectacular bruise around the small gash, but thankfully her eye didn't seem too swollen.

The hot water on her skin felt amazing, and Mia stood under the spray for ages letting it work its magic while she ran through today's to-do list in her head. She couldn't go into work, but she would definitely make some phone calls to find out how Tammy was doing and if any progress had been made finding out who had attacked her.

She shivered despite the heat as she remembered the unsettling feeling of being watched and then the terror as someone came running straight for her.

Suddenly the magic of the hot water was gone.

Her small, cozy house suddenly felt way too big and empty.

There were a lot of places that someone could hide, biding their time and waiting for the perfect opportunity to strike when she was alone and vulnerable.

Kind of like she was right now.

Quickly, she shut off the water and stepped out of the shower, snagging a towel and wrapping it around herself.

Maybe she would call a friend and see if someone was free to come and hang out with her today. It would worry them, but it was better than spending the day jumping at every little noise.

No.

She was being dramatic.

She was perfectly safe here. They didn't have any information on her attacker, and she had to assume they had gone after her simply because she was out there in the forest and they thought she had seen something. There was nothing to indicate that they knew where she lived or that they would try anything else.

Besides, she was positive that Julian had arranged for himself and the rest of the police department in town to drive down her street at least once an hour to keep an eye on everything just in case anything looked off.

Yes, she was safe here.

Perfectly safe.

Still, she jumped when she bumped into the bathroom door as she staggered when bending down to put on her sweatpants. She startled again when she turned on the upstairs hallway light, and her shaking fingers missed the switch the first time, her mind immediately processing that as someone had messed with the electricity. She paused at the bottom of the stairs, afraid that she would see someone come running at her the second she set foot in the kitchen.

By the time she did garner enough courage to open the kitchen door, her hands were sweaty, her breathing labored, and she was a hairsbreadth away from finding her cell phone and calling Julian regardless if it made her a coward or not.

Where was her cell phone?

It had been with her last night when she'd been attacked, but she had no idea if it had gotten lost out there, if her attacker had taken it, or if Julian had brought it back here with them. No, of course he would have brought it here, he wouldn't have gone to work today and left her without a means to contact someone if she felt worse.

She was just deciding if she should check the kitchen or make the trek back upstairs to her bedroom to see if it was up there when the doorbell rang.

It caught her by surprise, and she was already well past being on edge, and the sudden loud noise in the otherwise quiet house made her scream.

It wasn't a small scream either.

No, it was one of those from the bottom of your lungs scream for all you're worth kind of screams.

"Ma'am?" an anxious voice called out from the other side of the door. "Is everything okay?"

Mia relaxed slightly, she was letting what happened yesterday make her paranoid, and that was a place she didn't want to go back to. Hurrying to the door, she opened it to find a delivery guy on the doorstep, a bouquet of flowers in his hands. "Sorry about that, I'm a little jumpy this morning," she said sheepishly as she took the bouquet of forget-me-nots.

The man frowned, taking in her bruised face then looking behind her as though expecting to find whoever had attacked her standing in the house.

"Really," she added. "It happened last night, see, I have stitches." She indicated the neat little row of stitches Levi had put in.

"Okay then, well, if everything is okay." He nodded as though still unsure. "You have a nice day now."

"Thank you, you too," she said, watching as he walked away, then scanning the street. Nothing looked suspicious or out of place, and the sweet-smelling flowers in her arms went a long way to improving her mood. Julian was such a sweetheart, and she was so glad that they were finding their way back to one another. She couldn't wait for him to get back tonight so they could finally talk things through and then put the past behind them.

\* \* \* \* \*

10:44 A.M.

"What's wrong?"

Julian looked over at his brother Will. "Mia didn't answer when I called."

Will glanced at his watch. "It's not even eleven, and you only left two hours ago, she's probably still asleep."

"If I know Mia, she wouldn't have slept much past ten," he said. He hadn't wanted to leave her this morning, but he knew there was only so much fussing Mia could tolerate before she would have kicked him out anyway, and they did have to find whoever attacked her and kidnapped the boys and Tammy so he had to be here, he just didn't like it.

"Maybe she was in the bathroom. If she just woke up chances are the first thing she did was go and have a shower," Will suggested.

That was true, Mia did love long hot showers, and after what happened to her last night she probably would have gone straight into the shower as soon as she was up.

"Wait five minutes then call again," Will said, then snickered, "no, since it's Mia, you better wait fifteen minutes before calling again."

His brother's joking helped to ease some of the lingering tension and anxiety from last night, and Julian forced himself to focus. "You're right, I'm sure she's fine, I'll call her again soon."

"If you're really worried that this guy is going to go after her again, then we can figure something out, between us and Abe, Fletcher, Beau, and Sydney we can keep her covered."

"Thanks, I know you guys will help me keep her safe, I just wish I knew whether she was still in danger."

"The only way we can know that is to figure out who the kidnapper is. I wish you'd been able to see something last night."

"Me too, but all I saw was a shadowy figure and a truck. I couldn't even tell you if the guy was short or tall, or black or white, it was just too dark, and the light from the headlights behind him took away any definition I might otherwise have been able to see."

"We keep focusing on the guy, but did you notice anything distinguishing about the vehicle?"

Julian had gone over this in his head a hundred times, but each time he kept coming up with the same answer. "All I saw was a light-colored truck. I did shoot out the rear right tire so we should alert the mechanic in town and in the nearby towns to contact us if anyone comes in with a light-colored truck needing a new rear right tire."

"I'll make the calls, and you should check in on Mia."

While his brother left to go and make the calls, Julian picked up his own phone from his desk and prayed that Mia would answer this time. If she didn't, he would get in his car and drive over there to check on her. She didn't have a concussion, but she did have a nasty lump on her head, and while Levi hadn't said she'd need someone to watch over her the idea of leaving her alone didn't sit right with him. Then there were the psychological effects of what she'd been through, and Julian already knew she had issues processing and dealing with trauma.

"Hey," Mia's voice floated down the line. She didn't sound like she was in pain or freaking out being home alone after getting attacked, something he was sure would have been a trigger for her given everything Joshua had done to her.

"Just checking in," he said.

"I know," she said on a laugh. "Your note said you'd be checking in throughout the day.

"You didn't answer last time I called." Julian tried to keep the hint of reproach out of his tone but was pretty sure he failed.

"I must have been in the shower, then I wasn't sure where my phone was. It wasn't until I heard it ringing that I realized it was in the kitchen," Mia explained.

Of course she was in the shower, Julian couldn't help an eye roll, he was pretty sure she would live in the shower if she could. "What time did you get up?"

"After ten, I must have been exhausted, I never sleep that late."

"Your body needed the rest. How are you feeling?"

"My head hurts, and I'm still pretty tired. I don't think I'll end up doing much today."

"You're not supposed to be doing anything today," he reminded her.

"I know, but I want to check in with Lyle, and I want to get an update on Tammy, after that I'll probably take a nap."

"Definitely take a nap."

"Julian, do you ... do you have anything on the guy who attacked me?"

"No, I'm sorry, honey, but we'll find him." How many times had he said those same exact words to her when she was being stalked? Way more than he liked, and he hated they were back in that same place.

"Are you coming back here tonight?" she asked, sounding a little hesitant like she thought he was but wasn't positive.

"Do you really have to ask?"

"Just wanted to make sure," she said, and he could hear the smile in her voice. "I'll cook us dinner. Do you know what time you'll be back?"

"Don't cook dinner, you're supposed to be resting," he reminded her. "And I'm hoping I'll be home by six, that's the plan anyway."

"Okay, I'll have dinner on the table by six and hope you make it," Mia said with a finality that said further discussion on the topic was futile.

"I miss you already," he said, willing the next several hours away so he could go back to Mia's, hold her in his arms, kiss her, tell her how much he loved her, and never ever let her go again.

"Miss you too," Mia said, and he could hear her yawn.

"See you tonight, and go take a nap now, you need it."

"Yes, your highness," she said with a laugh. "Oh, I almost forgot, I meant to say thank you for …"

"All finished?" Will asked as he came back into the room.

"Hold on, honey, Will's back, I have to go."

"Okay, see you tonight."

"Make sure you go take your nap," he reminded her before hanging up. "Did you get anything yet?"

"I've called all the mechanics in the area. Too bad we can't just go after everyone in River's End who owns a light-colored truck and see if they have a busted tire."

"Maybe we can," Julian said thoughtfully. "The Miss Salsburys saw a light-colored truck at the attempted abduction of Rowan Douglas, and I saw the same sort of vehicle driven by whoever tried to grab Mia."

"That's not enough to get warrants to check every light-colored truck in the area," Will reminded him.

"We don't need one." He knew they didn't have enough to take this to court, but they needed to find that vehicle. The shot-out tire would identify the one they were looking for, and if CSU could find forensics to prove that the boys and Tammy had been transported in it, they would have enough to arrest their kidnapper.

"What are you thinking?"

"River's End is a small town, and no one likes to see anyone mess with one of the kids. You mess with them you mess with everyone. All we need to do is get a list of registered vehicles in this area that match our description so we know how many we're looking at and who owns them, then we ask them to let us take a look at their cars voluntarily. Anyone with nothing to hide will be all too happy to help out. That way, we can eliminate basically all of them leaving us with a few possibilities to look into further, or if we're really lucky, leaving us with only one person. The kidnapper."

Will nodded enthusiastically. "That could definitely work. You're right, everyone here would do anything to get his guy off the streets, going after the kids, and Mia, everyone wants him stopped."

"We need to start on this now," Julian said, already turning to his laptop. "This guy believes that Mia is a threat to him. He's not going to leave her alone forever if he believes that she saw something that will point us to him. She can't live with a death sentence hanging over her head again, and I can't either," he admitted. "What Joshua Graves did to her almost broke her, and it almost destroyed what we had. I just got her back, I'm not going to lose her again, I'm not going to let anyone else mess with what we have. We have to find him before he decides that he can't risk whatever Mia knows coming out."

Julian had never been more determined to do something in his life. He and Mia were getting their second chance, and he wasn't going to let anyone take it away from them.

He would kill anyone who tried.

* * * * *

5:37 P.M.

Mia woke with a start, certain that someone was standing over her watching her sleep.

Panicked, she looked around the living room only to find it empty.

What was going on with her?

Now she was getting that feeling of being watched while she was safe in her own home, in her own living room, taking a nap on her couch. It had been a while since she had been to a therapy session, maybe she needed to call her doctor and make another appointment. She had no idea what had brought on this sudden bout of paranoia, perhaps her dad's terminal diagnosis compounded by the fact that she and Julian were practically back together, but whatever it was, she had to get a handle on it now before it blew up and got out of control.

Shoving away the lingering unsettlement, Mia checked the time. Less than thirty minutes until Julian would hopefully be here, she should get up and make a start on dinner.

Feeling groggier than she had been before she'd taken her second nap for the day, Mia made coffee before she did anything else, that was a surefire way to clear away the cobwebs.

Mug of coffee in hand, she tackled the issue of dinner, she was tired and her head still hurt—she probably needed to take some more painkillers soon—so nothing fancy, but she had plenty of pasta in the pantry and in the freezer she had a container of her homemade tomato sauce, she could warm that up in a pot, cook the pasta, stir it through and that would be a quick and simple dinner that she could have ready to put on the table when Julian walked through the door.

Nostalgia ran through her as she bustled about the kitchen and waited for Julian. Her job had unpredictable hours just like his. She could do nothing but paperwork for days then work for days straight looking for someone who had gotten lost or was trapped somewhere. The time they had to spend together had been precious and she had loved sitting at the kitchen table eating dinner and talking, then cuddling on the couch together, before making love and falling asleep in each other's arms.

How had she survived the last eighteen months without him in her life?

The door opened, and a moment later she heard him behind her and turned to find him standing in the kitchen doorway. "Hey, Mia-bug, how was your day?"

"Fine, I slept for most of it." She drained the pasta and added it to the pot, stirring it through the sauce. "Did you make any progress?"

"Not really, but we're working on it."

That would have to be enough for now. Tonight wasn't about that anyway, tonight was about fixing what they had broken.

"I thought I told you not to make dinner," he tutted as he came up behind her, resting his hands on her shoulders and kissing her cheek.

"It's only pasta and a sauce I already had in the freezer," she said. "Not like it was any effort, and besides, I kind of like cooking for you."

Julian groaned, pulled the spoon from her hand, and turned her around so he could kiss her. When Julian's lips were on hers, her ability to think or focus on anything else fled and she lived and breathed the taste of him and the feel of him. Her hands curled into his shirt and his arms wrapped around her, pulling her closer. She closed her eyes as her body melted against his, kissing him like she had dreamed about so many times since he had walked away.

"We should stop," Julian said, his warm breath against her lips.

"I don't want to." Her hands moved to his face as she tried to draw his mouth back down to hers.

"Dinner will burn."

"I don't care."

"You didn't want us to do anything until we talked," he reminded her.

That managed to tug her out of her kiss-induced stupor. He was right, that was what she wanted, making out could wait. There would be plenty of time for it later tonight. "Okay, I don't like it, but you're right, we should talk first, and we can do that while we're eating."

"You're so cute when you pout," Julian said with a laugh as his thumb brushed against her bottom lip which she had jutted out just a little. "This is your plan remember. Talk first then make out."

"I know, it's just you're kind of irresistible, and besides you kissed me first," she shot back as she returned her attention to the stove.

"I know. You're kind of irresistible yourself." When he went to kiss her again, she waved him off.

"Oh, no, mister, you said you wanted dinner and dinner is what you're getting."

Julian groaned. "I'm regretting my decision now."

"Too late."

When she went to lift the heavy pot, Julian nudged her out of the way. "I'll do that, you go sit down."

Because she knew that Julian wasn't going to take no for an answer, she left him to dish up dinner while she sunk into a chair at the table and figured out exactly what she needed to say. She wanted to just get this over with, no more living in the past, no more regrets. She wanted to be sure of what the future held and let go of those last little doubts that said their issues were too big to overcome.

"You look so serious," Julian said as he set a bowl of pasta in front of her.

"Thinking about what we need to talk about."

He nodded, got his own plate, and joined her. "Floor is all yours, sweetheart."

"First off, I owe you an apology. Yes, I do," she said, holding up a hand to cut him off when he opened his mouth to protest. "You were right, I thought that I could handle everything on my own, I thought I had it all under control. I got angry when you said that I needed to get help. I felt so out of control while Joshua was tormenting me, and I wanted to pretend that once he was dead it was over and I could just go back to my life like none of it had ever happened. I resented you for not letting me do that. I shut you down every time you brought it up. I pretended that everything was fine even though deep down inside I knew it wasn't. When you left, and I realized what I had lost I finally realized that you were right. If you hadn't done it, then I don't know what would have happened, but I know it wouldn't have been good. So thank you." Her fear was that she would have fallen apart completely, dug herself into a hole she couldn't climb out of, and she was so thankful to Julian for saving her from that.

"Mia-bug, you don't owe me an apology, you had been stalked, abducted, shot, raped, and had to take a life to save your own. I understood why you didn't want to deal with it. I just couldn't stand by and watch you self-destruct without doing everything I could to stop it from happening."

"I know, Julian," she said, reaching across the table to cover his big hand with hers. She hated that she had caused him pain. "I'm sorry that I didn't spend more time thinking about how what happened affected you. I know how hard it was for you when he was stalking me and you couldn't stop it, I know how much you suffered when he took me, how scared you must have been. I should have realized that what happened affected both of us and acted accordingly instead of acting like it was all about me and I was the only one who had been traumatized. I'm sorry."

There were so many mistakes she had made, so many things she wished she had done differently. Yes, she knew she had been traumatized and dealing with a lot, but it wasn't an excuse to take it out on the one person who was suffering just as much as she was. So many times she had lost her temper with him when he'd pushed her to start dealing with what was happening, to accept that the hypervigilance and inability to sleep without nightmares were signs of post-traumatic stress disorder.

She, better than anyone else, knew why what happened would affect Julian the way it had, why he had to make sure she got help and the fact that she had hurt him cut her deeply. It was what had kept her from reaching out to him before now.

Tears pricked the backs of her eyes, but she fought them back because he didn't need to deal with her tears on top of everything else.

"I'm sorry, Julian, for everything that I did that hurt you. Can you forgive me?"

\* \* \* \* \*

6:12 P.M.

How could she ask him for forgiveness?

As far as Julian was concerned, Mia hadn't done anything wrong.

*He* was the one who had left, *he* was the one who hadn't been there for her as she dealt with the fallout from a horrific ordeal, and *he* was the one who had given up on her when she needed him.

"Mia, you have nothing to be sorry for."

Fire sparked in her eyes. "What happened wasn't all on you. It was both of us. You left, but I pushed you to it, and you know it."

He didn't know it, but he wasn't going to argue the point.

"Don't do that," Mia said, a hint of desperation sneaking into her tone. "Don't make this all about me because that's what broke us up last time. I acted like I was the only one affected and therefore entitled to do whatever I wanted, and you did the same until you couldn't anymore. If we want to change things, if we want to get back together then we have to look at this the way it is, not looking at it through eyes that are clouded by the past." Although there was sympathy in her eyes, there was also a sharpness that said she meant every word she was about to say. "I love you in a way I will never love another man, but if we don't sort this out now then we can't get back together. My heart couldn't take it," she finished softly, not bothering to hide her pain.

Julian dragged in a breath that felt like it scraped through his insides all the way down his windpipe and into his lungs.

This wasn't easy for him to talk about.

Only one person knew the entire story, and that person was Mia.

If there was one person he couldn't fool or brush off, pretend that he didn't know what they were talking about, it was her.

The woman who owned his heart.

The woman he had loved most of his life.

The only woman he would ever love.

"It's okay, Julian, I know how hard it is to talk about, trust me I do. But you have to." Mia stood, rounded the table, and planted herself right in his lap. She didn't say anything else, just rested her head on his shoulder, put her hand on his stomach, and gently stroked with her fingers.

In any other circumstances having her on his lap would have his body instantly responding, but all he felt now was a ball of dread that sat heavily in his gut.

Was this how Mia had felt every time he'd pushed her to talk to him or somebody else about what she had gone through?

If she had felt even one hundredth what he was feeling, how he regretted every single one of those times.

Because he believed that Mia meant it when she said that if they didn't deal with this now, any chance they had to fix this would be gone for good, he started speaking. "When Joshua was stalking you it brought back memories of the last time I had felt that helpless. I wanted so badly to save you because I hadn't saved her."

"Your mom's death wasn't your fault, Julian."

She'd told him that before, but he didn't believe her then, and he wasn't sure he believed her now. "I was there when she died."

"And it was an accident."

"We all knew that my dad had a drinking problem. He was drunk all the time, and he had started getting violent. I know he had seen and done things that changed him while he was serving, but hurting his wife wasn't okay."

"No, it wasn't," Mia agreed quietly.

"Will, Mom, and I never told anyone what was happening at home, as far as the rest of the town knew, we were just like all the other families, but we weren't. My dad's drinking was getting worse, he was drunk all the time, he lost his job, didn't even leave the house much anymore."

"You were just a kid, it wasn't your job to fix him."

"No, but we were a family, it was our job to protect each other, and I failed."

"You were nine," Mia reminded him.

"I know, but I still hear her screams, I still see the shock on her face and the realization of what was happening. I still feel like if I had just said something to someone, then she wouldn't be dead."

"She fell down the stairs," Mia said, touching her lips to his jaw.

"Because of my dad," he said bitterly. Over twenty years may have passed since the day his mother died, and he still hadn't been able to forgive his father. His dad had been drunk, as usual, and when his mother had decided to put a stop to it. They'd fought over the bottle of beer, they'd been standing at the top of the stairs, his dad had shoved his mother, intending just to get her to let go of the beer, but she'd lost her balance and fallen.

An accident.

His father hadn't been charged with anything, mainly because his nine-year-old self who had seen the whole thing simply said when asked that his mother had fallen and not given any more details.

He wasn't sure why he hadn't mentioned the argument.

Perhaps because he'd already lost his mother and whether he blamed his father or not, he didn't want to lose the only parent he had left.

To this day, Mia was the only other person who knew the

truth.

"I felt like—still feel like—I failed my mom. I didn't say anything to anyone, not even my aunt or uncle, about what was going on, and because of that, she died. An accident, yes, but one caused by my father's drinking. We were all too scared of him, and what he would do so we just let the drinking go on."

"He stopped after your mother's death though," Mia reminded him.

His father had not touched a drop of alcohol in twenty-one years to the best of his knowledge, but that didn't bring his mother back.

"I felt you slipping away from me. You weren't dealing with anything, you just wanted to pretend that it hadn't happened, that you hadn't been terrorized, that you hadn't been kidnapped, that you hadn't been assaulted, that you hadn't killed someone. I knew that you couldn't do that indefinitely. I couldn't lose you like I lost my dad. Being in the Marines changed him, I understood that, even as a child, but he lost himself, and you were losing yourself too. All I could see every time I looked at you was my mom falling down the stairs, and my dad's sobs, wracked with guilt and self-recrimination, and I knew I couldn't lose you the same way. I didn't want to leave you, Mia, I knew how much you needed me, but I couldn't stand by and do nothing and watch you disappear the same way my dad did. I'm sorry, I was a coward."

"No."

Mia said it so vehemently that his gaze snapped to hers to find her all but glaring at him.

"What you did was courageous and not at all easy. You loved me. You wanted to be there for me, you wanted me to get help. I was the one fighting you at every turn. I didn't leave you any other options. It was either leave or stay and watch me eventually crash and burn."

"How can you be so understanding? So forgiving? My leaving hurt you deeply."

"It did," she acknowledged, not flinching but looking him square in the eye. "Watching you walk away was like watching the only good thing left in my life leave. But it was what I needed, I hated you for a while, vowed I would never forgive you for abandoning me, but then I started therapy, I started processing and working through my issues, and then I realized just what it was you had done for me."

Julian just looked at her quizzically. Despite everything she had said, all he could see that he'd done was leave her when she was at her lowest point.

Mia smiled at him, lifted a hand to caress his cheek. "You loved me even when I made it near impossible to do so, you sacrificed your own happiness for me, you gave me what I needed even though I didn't know that I needed it. That is strength, that is courage, that is true love. Loving someone is about doing what's best for them even if they don't like it, and even if it's hard, and that's what you did for me. I'm so grateful every day that you're the man I fell in love with. I feel so lucky, so blessed, to be the woman that you fell in love with. It's time, Julian, it's time to let go of the guilt, your mom's death wasn't your fault, it was just a horrible accident, and what happened between us happened because of both of us, not just you. You love me, I love you, we want a future. I've accepted the reality of our situation, it's time for you to do the same. Please, so we can have everything we dreamed about."

Her imploring green eyes cracked through the guilt that had been growing inside him since he was nine years old. How could he hold onto anything that was causing her pain?

\* \* \* \* \*

6:29 P.M.

She saw the exact second when realization dawned, and he

finally set down the heavy bag of guilt he had been carrying around for so long.

And just like that, the heavy weight lifted from around her heart.

They were going to make it.

Unable to wait another second, Mia pressed her lips to his. Julian immediately tightened his hold on her and deepened the kiss. Passion bloomed in her stomach, curling out through her body until every inch of her felt hyper-sensitive.

She shifted on his lap, needing more than just his lips on hers. She needed all of him, everything that she had been yearning for these past eighteen long months.

"Julian," she whimpered against his lips. The plea was all she could manage to get out, her pulse raced, her body squirmed with desire. She wanted him upstairs and naked in her bed.

"Baby, I want you so much," he murmured as he stood with her in his arms.

"Not more than I want you. It's been so long." She trailed a line of kisses along his jaw as Julian carried her upstairs.

"Well, you don't have to wait any longer, I'm all yours, sweetheart. Forever." The love shining from the hazel eyes she knew so well made her own eyes tear up. She loved this man so much it had physically hurt to be apart from him.

"Forever," she echoed.

Julian set her on her feet in the bedroom then looked at her with that wicked smile that made her toes curl. "Strip," he ordered.

Mia shivered in delightful anticipation. Julian had always been so assertive in the bedroom, and she loved it. Since they had been together since they were young teens, she'd never been with another man, never even looked at one—okay, well, she wasn't blind so she could appreciate a hot guy, but she'd never felt the desire to sleep with another man.

With trembling fingers, she slipped her sweatshirt over her

head. Since she hadn't gone anywhere today, she hadn't bothered putting on a bra, and Julian sucked in a breath at the sight of her bare breasts. She'd always been a little lacking in confidence when it came to her breasts, they weren't big, but Julian seemed to like them and that was good enough for her.

When she took hold of the waistband of her sweatpants, Julian stopped her. "I think I want the honor of removing those tonight."

He knelt in front of her, touching a featherlight kiss to first one of her nipples and then the other, both of them pebbling, and she couldn't quite stop a whimper escaping when he didn't touch them further.

Instead, with excruciating slowness, he pulled her pants down her legs, leaving her standing there in nothing but a simple pair of pink cotton panties. Cupping both her cheeks in his hands, his fingers digging into her as he pulled her closer and buried his nose in the apex of her thighs, breathing deeply and making her body nearly explode with need.

"I missed this scent, I missed the feel of your skin." His fingers trailed up her spine making her shiver again. "I missed the way you chew on your bottom lip when your body is pulsing with need."

Mia realized she was chewing on her lip and deliberately released it, then glanced down at her mostly naked body. "This seems unbalanced."

Julian laughed. "Well, we wouldn't want any inequality in the bedroom," he teased with a wink and stripped off his shirt, boots, and jeans.

She took in the sight of him, naked he was a sight to behold. His legs were like tree trunks, his biceps bulged, his chest and abs looked like they had been sculpted out of stone. What she loved most about him was that his heart was bigger than any of his muscles, he cared, sometimes too much, but he was all hers, every delicious inch of him.

"Those panties have to go," Julian said as he scooped her up and set her on the bed, removing her underwear then touching her between her legs. "So wet," he murmured as he stretched out beside her.

"I don't think I can wait long," Mia said, already feeling like she was ready to combust with one more touch. In the first few months after her assault, she hadn't been able to even think about anyone touching her, but these last couple of months she'd started to get that restless feeling that said maybe she was ready for sex again. Only then she hadn't had anyone to have sex with.

. Now Julian was back in her life, and while there was definitely a lingering concern that perhaps she would freak out right in the middle of things, that fear was definitely outweighed by need.

Need to feel alive again.

Need to feel normal again.

Need to feel connected to someone again.

Not just anyone, she needed to feel connected to her husband, the man she loved, the man who could overwrite all the horrors Joshua Graves had imprinted upon her and replace all those awful memories with new ones. Precious ones.

"You're in luck, sweetheart, because I don't think I can wait long either," Julian whispered in her ear.

He moved above her, kissing her, balancing his weight on one elbow so his other hand was free to roam her body, leaving a trail of tingling goosebumps everywhere he touched.

Just when she thought she was going to die if he didn't touch her where she needed him to, he flipped them over so she was on top. Julian was almost always the one in control when they made love, but that he had let her take charge this time, knowing this was her first time since Joshua's assault and that she might be feeling apprehensive, made her love him all the more.

A man who knew what she was thinking, knew what she needed, without her having to tell him was something special, and she knew she was a lucky woman to have Julian in her life.

"It's all you, babe," Julian told her. "Tell me what you need."

"I need … I need you to touch me," she murmured.

Immediately, he reached up and claimed her breasts, kneading, teasing her nipples, making the ball of desire inside her grow.

Balanced on her knees, Mia took hold of his long, hard length, already anticipating that feeling of fullness she only ever experienced when Julian was buried deep inside her. She stroked him, enjoying the way he pulsed and twitched under her ministrations, and when she could tell by the tightening of his jaw that Julian wasn't going to be able to hold off much longer, she positioned him at her entrance and slowly took him inside her.

One of Julian's hands left her breasts to grip her hip, but he didn't urge her to go faster, just let her take her time, do things her way.

She waited for bad memories to hit her, but they didn't come, and once she had all of him inside her she began to move. Slowly at first, wanting to savor each and every second of this, but then as pressure built inside her she began to move faster. Up until just his tip was left inside her, then back down again until he was buried deep.

The faster she moved, the more desire and need bubbled inside her. She was close, so close, but not quite there yet and doubt began to creep in. Had what Joshua done to her ruined her ability to orgasm?

Sensing her distress, Julian asked, "What do you need, babe?"

"I need more," she told him.

The hand on her hip moved to touch the little bundle of nerves, and between him moving inside her and external stimulation she felt the first flicker of pleasure ignite. It grew quickly, and seconds later, she was screaming her release as it shot through her like a firework, setting alight every molecule of her body and her soul.

Julian's hands moved to grip her hips, and he thrust into her once, twice, three times before finding his own release.

As the last lingering waves of pleasure washed over her, Mia sank down against Julian, nuzzling his neck. "Thank you."

"Babe, don't thank me for that," he reprimanded softly as he pulled out of her and then tucked her closely against him. "Mia, we didn't do the whole protection talk before we did that."

"Oh," she said. She hadn't even realized that they hadn't used a condom. "I don't care. I haven't been with anyone since we broke up and I know you haven't either. I'm not on birth control, there wasn't any need for it, but we're still married and I don't care if we just made a baby." It was true she realized as she said the words, she and Julian had been talking about starting a family a few months before Joshua had started stalking her, then that had derailed things, but now that they were back together she couldn't wait to have Julian's baby growing inside of her.

She yawned, and Julian smoothed a hand down her back. "How about I clean you up, and you can get some sleep."

"What about dinner?" she asked, although the idea of sleep was an appealing one.

"I'd much rather hold you in my arms while you sleep," he told her.

Mia smiled. "You're so sweet sometimes."

"Only sometimes?" he teased as he gently rolled her over so he could climb out of bed. He returned a moment later with a warm cloth and wiped her down. Then he got back into bed, tucked the covers over both of them, and spooned her against him.

"I missed this," she said. Sleep tugged at her, but again she wanted to savor this moment, for a long time she had thought that it was over, that she and Julian would never be together again, but now here he was, in her home, in her bed, holding her in his arms.

It was perfection.

"I missed this too," he whispered back, and with a smile on her face she drifted off to sleep.

# OCTOBER 10<sup>TH</sup>

7:14 A.M.

Julian yawned and stretched as he woke up from the best sleep he'd had in over two years. The stress of the stalker, then Mia's response to her ordeal had messed with his sleep patterns, and while he could get by on little sleep, doing it night after night for months on end eventually took a toll. Then after he'd left, he'd missed Mia's small form in the bed beside him, her quiet snores, and the way she preferred to sleep snuggled against him. Now he had Mia back, and his subconscious mind had taken that as a cue to finally let go and relax and he'd slept like a rock all night.

When he turned his head, he saw that the bed was empty. Since he couldn't hear the shower running, Mia must have gotten up already and gone downstairs. If he knew her, and he did, then she was probably going all out cooking him breakfast.

Rolling out of bed, he found the clothes he'd been wearing the day before and threw them back on. Since he and Mia were back together, and they were technically still married because despite her sending him divorce papers Mia had never filed them, he wanted them to start living together again immediately. He could move in here—where they had lived when they were married—or she could move to his place, or they could find a new place for a new beginning, he didn't care. He just knew he wanted to sleep beside her every night, wake up to her smiling face every morning, and come home to her every evening, and he saw no good reason to wait to make that a reality.

He found her right where he expected to find her, in the

kitchen, whistling away as she tended to three separate frying pans on the stove.

Julian tried to school his features into a reprimanding frown but found he couldn't, she was just too cute wearing a pink frilly apron over her pajamas, with her feet in those ridiculous novelty star slippers.

"Morning," he said, leaning against the doorjamb.

Mia jumped and spun around, her brows knit together. "I forgot you thought it was fun to torment me by sneaking up behind me in that super stealthy way of yours so you could scare me."

Throwing back his head, Julian laughed, then walked over and wrapped an arm around Mia's waist, dragging her up against him and kissing her until she melted against him.

"You're supposed to be resting and taking it easy for a few days," he reminded her, "you should still be in bed asleep."

"I see fussy Julian is back this morning," she said, pushing lightly at his chest but he didn't release her. "We were in bed by seven last night and I got up at six, that's like eleven hours in bed. I think I'm fully rested."

"Yeah, but not all of those hours were spent sleeping," he reminded her with a grin. He'd made her come five more times after they'd made love that first time. She'd come on his fingers, his mouth, and with him buried inside her.

Mia rolled her eyes. "Men." She huffed as she deftly twisted out of his hold and returned her attention to the stove where she was cooking bacon, eggs, pancakes, and he could see the waffle maker on the counter.

She was going all out.

For him.

And now he felt like a jerk for deliberately startling her and then annoying her by telling her she wasn't up to doing anything too strenuous. Which given that he had been bragging about how many times they'd had sex made him a major hypocrite.

"Hey, I'm sorry," he said, snagging her elbow and turning her back into his embrace. "I just worry about you. How is your head feeling this morning?"

She softened and nestled her head against his chest. "It's feeling better, I hardly have a headache at all, and I want to go back to work, but I know your worrywart of a cousin won't clear me to go back until at least tomorrow."

He knew how much Mia hated to just sit around and do nothing. The few vacations they'd managed to take between his time in the military, her job, and his, she'd struggled just to relax and chill. She'd filled up every second of the time with activities.

"I know, babe," he said sympathetically, kissing the top of her head. "But it's only one more day."

"Easy for you to say," she muttered, but her arms came up to wrap around his waist, holding onto him tightly. "I just hate the idea of not being out there searching if another kid goes missing today."

On the other hand, he was relieved to have her out of commission and safe at home should another search be needed. He wanted her out of harm's way and couldn't get out of his head the image of her lying unconscious on the ground just moments away from being abducted.

"Today will go fast," he assured her, "and tonight we can play." He waggled his eyebrows to make her laugh and was rewarded with a giggle.

"So when are you moving back in?" she asked as she moved out of his arms and started removing food from the stove, dishing it up onto two plates.

Pleased that she was already on the same page he was, he grabbed glasses and a bottle of sparkling water from the fridge. "Today. Well, I'll at least stop by my place before I come here tonight and pack up some clothes and toiletries." Not that there really was much else, he'd left everything here when he'd moved out, and his house was filled only with a few pieces of furniture, a few family photos, and his personal belongings.

"Before you come *home* tonight," Mia corrected as she took the plates to the table and sat down.

"Before I come home tonight," he echoed. His house had never felt like a home, it had just been the building he lived in. This little house he and Mia had bought together when they first got married had always been his home.

"Oh, why don't you bring over some of the flowers you sent me and we can put them on the table," Mia said, waving a hand at the vases of flowers on the counter.

He was already reaching for them when what she had said registered in his brain. "What? The flowers I sent you?"

Mia laughed. "I meant to thank you for them earlier but somehow I kept getting distracted. Did you think because you didn't include a card that I didn't know they were from you?"

Dread settled in his stomach like a lead balloon. "Mia, I didn't send you any flowers."

Confusion covered her face. "Yes, you did." She pointed again to the four vases of flowers on the counter. There was a bouquet of bluebells, Mia's favorite flowers, a bouquet of an array of all-pink flowers, a single white rose, and a bouquet of forget-me-nots. All the flowers looked fresh like they had been delivered within the last several days.

"No, honey, I didn't." That lead balloon in his stomach was growing.

"But ... but ... but ..." Mia stammered, fear coating every word.

Breakfast forgotten, he joined her at the table, pulling a chair around so he was right in front of her, his hands resting on her knees. "Mia, when did you get the first bouquet?"

"That night that Devin went missing. They were there in the locker room when I finished changing my clothes, the evidence bag with my clothes in it was gone and the flowers were in their place. I thought you had brought them to me. You were acting so oddly when you found me and Devin, and I thought it was because you wanted to maybe talk to me about getting back together. I mean you knew I was there, so I thought you must have brought them with you, and then you texted to say goodnight, and I just thought …" she trailed off, doubt filling her forest-green eyes.

"Mia, I *had* been thinking about us, and I *did* want us to get back together, and when I saw you that night it did make those feelings grow. When I sent the text, it was because I wanted to see if you were interested in seeing if we could fix things, but I didn't bring you flowers."

"Then who did?" she whispered.

"I don't know." And that terrified him.

All the color drained from Mia's face, and he quickly scooped her up and sat down with her on his lap, afraid she was about to pass out. "Julian, I didn't realize at the time, but the flowers are what *he* sent me. First it was the bluebells, then the pink flowers, then the single long-stemmed white rose, and then the forget-me-nots. It was so long ago, and there were so many other things he sent in between, and I forgot, but these were the flowers Joshua sent me when he was stalking me."

And now it looked like someone else was stalking her.

His hold on her tightened as though his arms were enough to keep away any potential threat, but he hadn't been able to save her last time, and he might not be able to save her this time.

\* \* \* \* \*

8:00 A.M.

"It's okay, honey, we'll figure this out," Julian told her, stooping to kiss her forehead before he resumed pacing the room.

Just how he thought he was going to do that Mia had no idea.

He hadn't been able to last time, no one had. It wasn't until

Joshua had come to her house, pretending to be the plumber—
who he had killed to steal his truck—that she learned the identity
of the man stalking her. Thankfully, a neighbor had seen the
abduction and called it in, with the description of her kidnapper
and the dead body of the plumber, Julian was able to ID Joshua
and track down where he had taken her. By then she had already
been sexually assaulted, shot, and killed Joshua, fleeing into the
forest where she was eventually found.

How could this be happening to her again?

And why hadn't she noticed sooner that the flowers were the
same ones her stalker had sent her?

At least now she knew why she kept getting that unsettling
feeling that she was being watched.

Because she *was* being watched.

Mia looked at Julian, needing him right now, but he was in full-
on cop mode, she could tell by the stiffness in his posture and the
tightness of his mouth. There was no point in trying to talk to
him; all he would give her were more of his cop platitudes.

The doorbell rang, and she jumped off the couch. Was that her
stalker? Was he here?

"Relax, Mia-bug." Julian's hands rested on her shoulders as he
took a moment to work some of the tension out of her neck. "It's
only Abe."

"Abe?" She tilted her head to the side to give Julian better
access.

"To talk about your situation."

"My situation?" Mia did not want to think of this as a situation.

"We'll figure this out," Julian said again as he kissed her cheek
and left the living room to let Abe in.

Alone, Mia immediately began to fidget. She wasn't much of a
pacer, when she was stressed she usually fiddled with anything
that was close to her hands. Right now, there was nothing within
reach so she wandered back to the sofa and began to twirl the frill
on one of the throw pillows.

"Hey, Mia," Abe said as he and Julian entered the room. Abe was a big guy with a bushy red beard and piercing hazel eyes, she'd been a little intimidated by him when they were kids, but he had a big heart, and ever since he had gotten together with Meadow he had mellowed even further.

"I'd say it's nice to see you, but …" she trailed off, shooting him a small smile.

Abe grinned. "No offense taken."

Julian sat beside her on the couch and Abe took one of the armchairs, and although she knew they weren't here to interrogate her, she couldn't help but feel like they were. She remembered the hours she had spent down at the precinct with Abe or Julian or one of the other guys as she went over every single detail of her life as they tried to figure out who was stalking her.

"Julian said you got some flowers," Abe said, easing into things no doubt because she was his cousin's wife. Although knowing Abe, he was probably surprisingly gentle with everyone whose path was unlucky enough to cross his in his role as sheriff.

"I thought they were from Julian," she said, twisting the frills around her fingers so tightly it hurt, anything to distract her from her fear.

"When did you get the first ones?" Abe asked.

"The night that Devin was missing. Julian was there, he found us in the forest, and he was acting kind of odd. When I saw the flowers I thought they were his way of reaching out," she explained.

"Where were they?"

"In the locker room, right with my stuff," she replied. "My clothes in the evidence bag were gone so I assumed Julian came in to get them, left the flowers, then headed to the hospital to check on Devin."

"Julian?" Abe looked to his cousin.

"I did go in and take the evidence bag with Mia's clothes, and I intended to talk with her about us, but she wasn't there," Julian

150

said.

"Did you see anyone else in there?" Abe asked.

"No," Julian said. "The whole search and rescue team was there, along with at least two dozen people from town. Everyone wanted Devin Deville found safe and sound."

"So we have a lot of suspects," Abe said, sounding frustrated. But no one was more frustrated than she was right now.

A glance at Julian and the stark terror he was trying to hide, but that she could see lurking deep in his hazel eyes, reminded her that he was just as affected by this as she was. How could either of them live through this nightmare again?

"Besides the flowers, has anything else strange been happening?" Abe asked her.

"Well," she hesitated, not wanting the guys to think she was crazy.

"Everything is important right now," Julian reminded her. Prying the pillow from her hands, he took both of hers between his and began rubbing them lightly.

"Okay," she agreed. "I've been feeling like someone is watching me when I've been out searching for those kids. It's like I'm not alone, I'll hear what sounds like a twig snapping or something, but when I look, no one is there. No matter how hard I look I can't see anyone else out there with me, and yet at the same time, I can't shake that feeling of eyes following me wherever I go."

"When did this feeling of being watched start?" Abe asked.

"The night I was looking for Devin."

"Was it every time you were out there?" Abe asked.

"Yes, each time I went out there looking for the kids, and when we were doing a training exercise, but the night Tammy was missing was the only time I actually saw anyone. The rest of the time it was just a feeling."

"Why didn't you say anything to me about it?" Julian asked, looking like a hurt little puppy.

"Because I thought I was imagining it. I thought it was the stress of everything going on with my dad. I felt like I was losing my mind, but I did not honestly believe that anyone was watching me. At worst, I thought maybe it was the kidnapper who was out there keeping an eye on things. If I had known that someone was targeting me I would have told you. I promise," she added.

"Okay," he said, his face softening. "I don't want you anywhere on your own until we get this sorted out. I don't want to take any chances this time around."

Her stomach dropped as a thought occurred to her. "What if Joshua wasn't really dead? What if he's come back to get me?" Panic coursed through her at even the notion of having to face that man again after everything he had done to her. The only way she had managed to get through it was because of the peace of mind of knowing that he was dead and could never hurt her again.

"Relax, sweetheart." Julian moved so he was closer and pulled her against his side, tucking her head under his chin, his hand lightly rubbing her shoulder. "He's dead. I saw his body. He's definitely dead, he can't ever hurt you again."

"But someone *is* stalking me." This didn't feel real, and yet there didn't seem to be any way to pretend that it wasn't. Then she remembered something. An all-consuming terror filled her. "Julian," she gulped.

"What?" Concerned eyes looked down at her.

"Last night, I was taking a nap while I waited for you to come home. I woke up maybe twenty minutes before you got here. When I woke up I could have sworn that someone was watching me. What if there was? What if he was here in the house watching me while I slept?" The idea of it left her feeling completely and utterly violated.

"You don't leave my sight, ever, for any reason, until we find this guy," Julian said fiercely, dragging her onto his lap. Protectiveness oozed out of his every pore, and she certainly wasn't going to argue with that. She was trained in search and rescue, she was strong, independent, knew how to use a gun, and had spent years learning self-defense, but she wasn't stupid. She was safer when she was with Julian, who had served in the Marines before becoming a cop, and she wasn't going to play the I can take care of myself and don't need anyone card.

She wanted to live.

Besides, the only place she felt safe was in Julian's arms. She'd just got him back, and she wasn't going to let anyone—and certainly not some obsessed stalker—take him away from her.

Or take her away from him.

\* \* \* \* \*

11:19 A.M.

Mia laughed at something Poppy said, and Julian felt a part of himself relax. As awful as this was and as much as he hated that Mia had to go through this all over again, she was okay.

And she'd stay okay.

He wouldn't let this new stalker lay a finger on her, and he would make sure that once they had this guy in custody, both he and Mia got some help processing it.

Both he and Mia had been blessed with a second chance, and often in life you didn't get the opportunity for a do-over, there was no way he was letting anyone or anything mess this up. Not even himself and Mia. He had stood by and not done anything to try to put a stop to his father's drinking and anger problems, and it had cost him his mother. He had walked away from Mia even though he loved her with every fiber of his being because he couldn't make that same mistake again and let someone he loved pay the price for his silence. This time, he and Mia were going to deal with things as a team.

"You ready?" Abe asked him, joining him at the door that led to the precinct's foyer where Mia was keeping Poppy company.

Julian had insisted that she come with him to the station and she hadn't protested. She was upset, but she was still able to think clearly, and she knew that she was safer here—even if she didn't like the idea of no privacy until they found out who was watching her and sending her flowers—than she was at home where someone may or may not have broken in and watched her sleep.

Despite the fact he knew she was perfectly safe here—he, Abe, Will, Fletcher, Sydney, and Beau were all here—and she and Poppy both knew to alert them immediately if someone showed up, even if it was someone they knew and thought they could trust, he still didn't like the idea of not having her within his line of sight. They were only going to be in the conference room while they worked out a plan to identify Mia's stalker, but that was three empty rooms between him and Mia and that felt like too many.

"Yeah, ready," he said with a last glance at Mia who was chattering away with her friend and didn't notice him watching her. He and Abe had gone through every second of every day of the last week with her this morning and spoken with her friends who didn't remember seeing anyone following her or watching them the day of their lunch, and now it was time for him and his colleagues to work their magic and find the stalker.

He and Abe joined Will, Fletcher, Sydney, and Beau in the conference room where someone had already written up everything they knew so far, and the sense of déjà vu he got from seeing his wife's life up on a board like she was just some victim in a case hit him hard. Last time he had nearly lost Mia, what would he do if this time he did?

Shaking off that mode of thinking, he didn't want to jinx things, Julian took a seat. "First thing we need to do is look into the flowers, see if we can find who ordered them. Even if he paid with cash, this is a small town so the florist should recognize them, and if no one does then we know we're looking for someone who doesn't know Mia personally."

Abe nodded his agreement. "When we finish up here Fletcher

and Sydney will go and look into that."

"All those missing kids they were just a distraction," he said. "That's why he was able to change from boys to girls so easily. He didn't care who they were, probably just took them because they were easier than trying to deal with an adult. He drugged them so they weren't any trouble, then took them out into the forest because he knew it would get search and rescue involved."

"You think the goal was to get Mia out there alone so he could nab her?" Will asked.

"Yes." That was exactly what he thought. Given that the abductions didn't appear to be committed by anyone with a vested interest like they had originally thought, and the fact that the children weren't harmed, the only logical conclusion that he could come to was that they were simply a tool the kidnapper had used to attempt to achieve his goals.

"She said she felt like someone was watching her while she was out searching for the kids," Abe added. "Beau and Will, you two go and talk to Lyle and get a list from him of every person who was at all the searches so we can cross-reference them. We particularly need to know who was at the first search because someone left Mia flowers."

"Wasn't it only people from town at the searches?" Will asked.

"That we know of," Abe replied.

"Just because it's someone who lives in River's End doesn't mean it can't also be Mia's stalker. Joshua Graves worked at the supermarket and had lived here for going on four years before he started stalking Mia," Julian reminded them.

"What about the mechanic angle?" Beau asked. "Did we get any reports of cars needing rear tires replaced?"

"No, so this guy either did it himself, or he has hidden the truck away and doesn't intend to use it again," Abe replied.

"Anyone in town buying tires that would match the type of vehicle we're looking for?" Sydney asked.

"No. If he changed it himself he must have used the spare,"

Abe said.

"So the mechanic thing has been a bust so far. What about our list of registered pale-colored trucks in the area?" Fletcher asked.

"We have one, and we've started contacting people on it. So far, everyone we've asked has been happy for me to come and examine their vehicle," Will explained.

"How are we going to keep Mia safe?" Julian asked. While he wanted this guy caught and off the streets, his focus was on making sure Mia remained unharmed. There was no way she could go through this stress again. No way *he* could go through this stress again. And he was very afraid that their relationship couldn't withstand the stress of another stalker.

"She doesn't go anywhere alone," Abe said.

"Of course," Julian said, fighting the urge to roll his eyes.

"Beyond that, all we can do is find this guy," Abe said, sympathy shining from his hazel eyes. Abe knew all too well what it was like to have some psychopath stalking the woman you loved.

"You're staying with her, right?" Will asked.

"Yeah, I told her before I found out about the flowers that I was moving back in, so she's safe with me at night, even if this guy broke in once already. During the day she needs to be here at the precinct."

"I'm not sure she's going to go for that," Sydney said.

"She can go to work, Julian can just go with her." Abe looked thoughtful, and the gleam in his cousin's eye said he probably wasn't going to like whatever Abe was ruminating on.

"You want me to play bodyguard?" It wasn't that he was opposed to the idea, he wanted to go wherever Mia went, wanted her where he could see her at all times, he just wasn't sure that it could work. River's End was a small town without a lot of crime, but there was still crime, and with this case dominating their time and resources it meant they would be stretched thin dealing with anything else that cropped up.

"I was just thinking that this all circles back to search and rescue. The missing kids were used as a way to attempt to isolate her and two of the bouquets of flowers were left for her there. If she's there I think we have a better chance at drawing this guy out," Abe said.

"You want to use Mia as bait?" he demanded.

"No, I want her to attempt to live her life as normally as possible, both for her mental health as well as yours, and I think in doing that, there's the added bonus that we tip this guy's hand, encourage him to make his move in a way we can control the outcome. And I want you there with her, every day, don't let her out of your sight," Abe told him.

Like he had any intention of doing that.

He was about a hairsbreadth away from handcuffing himself to her.

Then something occurred to him. "Rex Stevens was there watching after the second rescue. I kissed Mia, and she said she received the long-stemmed white rose that day. Rex has only been in town a month, he drives a light-colored truck, and Mia said he asked her out several times even after she already turned him down and told him she was married. He would have had a reason to be out in the forest during the searches and could have been following Mia. He knows where she lives, it's possible he found out about the flowers Joshua sent her that day he was here reporting the theft of his laptop, remember he was here alone for a while because we got called out on the Peterson fire, so he could have gotten into the archives. And he's a trained paramedic, which means he would know how much Rohypnol to give the boys to knock them out but not cause them any long-term side effects."

\* \* \* \* \*

6:52 P.M.

"I don't know how I can be this tired, all I did was sit around all day and talk with Poppy," Mia said as Julian pulled into her driveway. It felt like she had spent the entire day out hiking through treacherous terrain instead of hanging out with her friend then helping Julian pack up his things to bring to her house.

"You're still recovering from a head injury," Julian reminded her as he turned off the engine. "Don't get out of the car till I come around."

It wasn't until that moment that it really hit her.

She had another stalker.

Someone had been following her and sending her flowers. Someone had lured her out into the forest alone under the guise of searching for a kidnapped child, then they'd knocked her out and been preparing to abduct her.

*Would* have abducted her if Julian hadn't shown up.

"Hey, you okay?" Julian had rounded the car, opened her door, and unsnapped her seatbelt. He took her chin between his thumb and forefinger and tilted her face so she was looking at him.

"It's just … everything kind of sank in when you said that. It's really happening, it's not a bad dream, someone is stalking me, and you're now my bodyguard." She didn't want to be thinking it—and she knew it wasn't true—but she couldn't help but feel that things had changed between them. Now they weren't just a couple working on rebuilding their relationship, they were a bodyguard and a victim.

"I'm not just your bodyguard, Mia, I'm the man who loves you more than anything else in this world." Regret and guilt filled the handsome face that looked back at her. "I promise you this time I'll do a better job of keeping you safe."

Sadness filled her heart. "Oh, Julian." She took his face between her hands, her fingertips caressing the features she knew so well she could recognize him in the dark just by touch. "It wasn't your fault. I didn't ever blame you for Joshua kidnapping me. We didn't know he was dangerous at that stage, and he killed someone to get to me. If you could, I know you would protect me from ever being hurt by anyone again."

"I wish I could take away all the pain he caused you." Julian took a lock of hair that had escaped her braid, twirled it around his finger then tucked it behind her ear.

"Don't you know that you do?" She let her fingers trail down his cheek so her thumb could brush across his bottom lip. "Every time you kiss me you make me forget." She moved her hand to cover one of his. "Every time you touch me." She lifted her hand and placed it on his chest, right over his heart. "Your love heals every hurt. I love you, Julian. Always and forever."

"Aww, honey, you are my everything. I hate that …"

She cut him off by pressing her finger to his lips. "It's done. We both messed up, but we're here now, together, and this time we know what mistakes not to make again. Take me inside, Julian."

His gaze focused, and she lost her Julian to cop Julian, but she wasn't going to complain, he was tasked with her protection, and he would blame himself if anything happened to her.

After scanning the street and the yard, he helped her out of the car, closed her door and locked the vehicle, before positioning her slightly in front of him as they walked down the front path. At the door, he handed her his backup weapon and told her to wait on the porch while he cleared the house.

Mia waited anxiously for him to return, not because she thought she was incapable of defending herself but because she didn't want this to be real. She wanted to wake up in bed, with Julian wrapped around her, and find that the last twelve hours had all been a nightmare.

"All clear," Julian said as he returned. He bustled her inside and locked up, setting the alarm before turning to face her. "What do you want to do tonight?"

She just arched a brow.

Did he really have to ask?

More relaxed now that he knew they were safely locked in for the night, he shot her that grin that was guaranteed to melt the panties off a nun. "You don't want to eat something first, watch a movie?"

"Are you telling me you *don't* want to go straight upstairs?"

"Nope, just trying to be a gentleman."

"Well, we had dinner while we were packing up your things—which speaking of, are still sitting in your car—and I can think of a dozen things a whole lot more fun than watching a movie that we could do in the bedroom."

"First, we had a couple of slices of leftover four-day-old pizza, that isn't dinner. Second, it would be presumptuous of me to assume you want to go and make out after the day you've had. And third, you might not want to eat anything else tonight, but I do." The way his eyes met hers and then dipped further down her body, before running his tongue across his bottom lip had needy desire flaming inside her.

"You better be prepared to back up all that talk with some action," she said, shooting him a sultry smile.

Julian groaned, then the next thing she knew, she was over his shoulder and he was running up the stairs. Mia squealed and clutched at his shirt, then giggled as he reached her bedroom and tossed her onto the bed, making her bounce on the mattress.

"How did you get even prettier in the months we were apart?" he asked as he stood beside the bed looking down at her with awe on his face.

"How did you get sweeter? I don't remember you saying so many nice things to me before." She meant it to be teasing, but sadness covered his features.

"Because I took you for granted. We'd been together for so long, and I thought you would always be there. Having to learn to live without you made me realize just how good I'd had it. Now that I have you back, I'm never going to make that mistake again.

I'm going to make sure that every day for the rest of our lives I tell you how much you mean to me."

Tears blurred her vision, and she knew she was grinning like an idiot. "That's beautiful."

"*You're* beautiful," he corrected. Then that sexy gleam was back in his eye. "Now, I want you out of those clothes because you are never more beautiful than when you're coming."

Mia laughed and quickly stripped out of her jeans, sweater, and underwear, and by the time she settled back onto the mattress, Julian was naked and looking like he was ready to devour her.

"Dessert time," he murmured as he stretched out over her.

His tongue touched the tip of her nipple to wet it and then he blew on it, making her shiver as her nipple pebbled. When he took it into his mouth, she moaned and subconsciously lifted her chest off the bed, silently pleading for more.

He ministered to first one breast and then the other, sucking and nipping, and by the time he kissed his way down her stomach and settled between her legs she was almost mindless with desire.

That moment when his mouth finally touched her where she was aching for him she left the planet, floating up into space, higher and higher with each lick of his tongue. A finger slid inside her, and then another, and she was practically out of the universe now.

Her hips rocked as his mouth sucked and his fingers stroked and then she burst into a million sparks as pleasure flamed through her. Julian didn't let up, dragging out her orgasm for so long that by the time she finally floated back down to earth she was sure she wouldn't be able to move for the rest of the night.

"Told you," Julian said.

All she could do was arch a brow in a silent question.

"You're never more beautiful than that moment when you lose yourself in your pleasure."

"You're pretty beautiful yourself you know," she said, renewed energy flowing through her veins as she looked at his long, hard length. "And I'm pretty sure it's my turn now."

"Is it now?"

"Oh, yeah." Kneeling up, she pushed on Julian's shoulders to get him to lie down, and then she wrapped a hand around him and grinned when he sucked in a breath. She knew just what he liked and began to move her hand, keeping her hold light and her strokes slow. His eyes fixed on her hand watching it as it went from his tip down to his base and back up again. When she could see in his eyes that he was starting to lose control she increased her speed and tightened her hold on him.

Just as she was sure he was about to come, he growled, reached over, and grabbed her wrist, flipping them so she was lying beneath him, and buried himself inside her with one thrust.

"Want to come inside you," he grunted as he thrust harder and faster.

Julian reached between them and touched her and although she was sure that she wouldn't be able to come again after the mind-blowing orgasm he'd just given her she could feel another building inside her.

She came a split second before he did and she knew it was because he wasn't going to allow himself to find his release before she found hers.

This one hit her even harder than the last, and by the time she regained her ability to think, tears were trickling down her cheeks. How had she lived so long without him? How had she allowed anything to come between them? This man was her everything, and she hoped that their little family would soon include a baby.

# OCTOBER 11$^{\text{TH}}$

10:34 A.M.

"Good morning, Rex," Julian said as he strode into one of the two small interview rooms at the River's End Police Station. He was beyond ready to get some answers. Seeing the fear in Mia's forest-green eyes when she got up this morning to remember all over again that someone was fixated on her was enough to fuel his guilt into overdrive, and the only thing that was going to assuage it was finding who was stalking her.

"What's this all about?" Rex demanded.

Despite the several attempts they'd made yesterday to get into contact with Rex Stevens, all they had been able to do was leave some messages and hope that he showed up on his own. He hadn't been at his house, and Lyle hadn't seen him all day. Julian had been starting to think the man had realized his cover was blown and disappeared. Then Rex had arrived at the station about ten minutes ago with a glare on his face and an attitude to rival any hormonal teenage girl.

Ignoring Rex's question, Julian took a seat on the opposite side of the table and took his time arranging his papers. They weren't really anything he needed, he already knew what questions he would be asking, but he wanted to give the impression that they had some sort of physical evidence pointing to Rex as Mia's stalker and the kidnapper.

"What made you decide to move to River's End?" Julian asked.

Rex's eyes widened then narrowed. "I needed a change."

"Oh." He nodded thoughtfully. "I thought it might have been

the charges."

Red bloomed on Rex's cheeks. "Those were dropped," Rex said through gritted teeth.

"Ah, yes." He smiled agreeably. "That's right, I'm sure it was just a misunderstanding."

"It wasn't a misunderstanding," Rex huffed. "My ex left me, took my kid with her, I wasn't going to let that happen."

"So you started stalking her?"

"No, not her, my son. No way I was letting her take him away from me."

"But he wasn't your son, was he?" Julian already knew the answer, the research he and Abe had done had told them everything they needed to know.

"I didn't know that. Thought it was my kid, I was there for him every day for the first nine years of his life, then she just dropped that bombshell." From the steam that was practically shooting from Rex's ears, he was still furious about the betrayal. "Soon as she proved I wasn't the father, I didn't have a leg to stand on, and she took the boy and disappeared."

"That was a rough deal," he clucked sympathetically. "So you decided to move to River's End. Mia play any part in that decision?"

Rex's eyes narrowed. "You mean because she offered me a job?"

"I mean because of Mia's green eyes and blonde hair." The look he shot the older man was sharp. He'd seen a picture of Rex's ex and the similarities between her and Mia couldn't be ignored. Rex was jilted by his ex, who had lied about him being the father of her child, then he moves to River's End, and less than a month later Mia starts receiving bouquets of flowers.

"What is this about?" Rex over-enunciated each word. "Why are you asking me about Mia?"

"Someone has been sending her flowers."

"So?"

165

"Someone knocked her unconscious and was about to put her in a truck when I found her."

"What does that have to do with me?"

"You tell me."

"Nothing. It has nothing to do with me. And I don't know why you would think it does."

"You've asked Mia out. More than once I understand."

"Yeah, so what? She's a beautiful woman. You jealous, Black?"

"Jealous? Nope. Mia is my wife, and she turned you down flat, no less than six times. You have trouble understanding the word no, Rex?"

Rex just glowered.

"I understand that you have made a habit of making sure that your search area is always next to Mia's. Any reason for that?"

A one-shouldered shrug was his only response.

"Were you watching her while she was looking for those missing children?"

"I was doing my job," Rex seethed.

"So it was merely a coincidence that the night she was attacked you were uncontactable and out there in the bordering search grid?"

"My radio wasn't working. You make it sound so sinister. I thought Mia was hot, yeah, so what? I didn't attack her and I didn't send her any flowers."

Julian was about to push harder, but there was a knock on the interview room door. Since he knew that no one would interrupt if there wasn't a good reason to, he stood and left, leaving Rex glaring after him.

"What?" he asked Abe who was waiting for him on the other side of the door.

"Another kid was just reported missing."

"I thought we told parents not to let their kids go anywhere alone," he said. Even though the kids appeared to be used purely to lure Mia out into the forest alone, it didn't preclude one from winding up hurt or even dead.

"It's Lucy Barrow. Looks like she was lured off her farm."

"How long has she been missing?"

"We're not sure. She was out playing all morning, mother went to check on her, and she was already gone."

Julian swore under his breath. "So Rex could have stashed the kid somewhere and then come down here hoping to throw us off his back."

"Possibility," Abe agreed.

Turning, he opened the door. "You're free to go, Rex. Don't leave town."

"What? Just like that?" Rex stormed across the small room. "So you just brought me in here to ruin my day?"

"Yeah, Rex, the whole world revolves around you," he muttered. "Get out of here." If another kid was missing they needed everyone that they could to be out there searching.

Everyone except Mia.

But if she was going to stay here, he certainly wouldn't leave her here with the man he suspected was stalking her. He would just have to hope that Rex was obsessed enough with Mia not to skip town.

Since he knew that Rex would find out anyway and he may as well gauge his reaction, Julian said, "Another kid is missing. Mia is still recovering so Lyle will be running the search. You better get over there and see what he needs you to do."

Rex's eyes darkened, but all he did was nod and turn on his heel to leave.

"Oh, Rex, I noticed you're driving a rental. Any reason why?" he called out to the man's back.

Rex paused but didn't turn around. "Engine troubles."

"You still like him as the stalker?" Abe asked once Rex had left.

"Yep. Which is why I don't want him here with Mia while we go searching. Rex will be out there along with the rest of us, and

I'll tell Lyle to make sure he puts someone with him so he can't circle back here to get her." Mia wasn't going to like being sidelined, but he liked the idea of leaving her alone even less. She should be safe enough here, he'd tell her and Poppy to lock the doors and not let anyone in, and he'd make sure both women were armed, and Rex would be otherwise occupied. Still, it went against his every instinct not to stay here with her.

"Is it him? Did he say something incriminating?" Mia asked, obviously having seen Rex leave.

May as well get this over with. "No, honey, he didn't say anything I can use."

"Then why did you let him go?"

"Because another kid has gone missing."

Mia gasped, guilt filling her eyes before she shoved it away, the professional in her taking over. "We have to get over there."

"You're not going."

Her brow scrunched. "What? Why?"

"Why? Because you are the intended target and we're not going to hand you over to him on a silver platter. You and Poppy will stay here, lock the door, and wait for me to get back."

"This is my job, Julian, and Levi said I could go back to work today. The only reason I'm not already there is because I was working here today, so I could stay with you, and you could still work. If a child is out there then I need to be there." She had planted her hands on her hips and was giving him her best overly patient face.

As much as he appreciated her dedication to her job, her safety was his number one priority, and he had to play hardball as much he hated causing her pain. "Mia, this is about you. If you go out there then everyone else is in danger. Rex knows that we're onto him, he could start becoming unhinged, I think everyone—including you—is safer if you stay here."

"I hate that you're making sense," she muttered, deflating.

"I know you do, but at least we're making progress, as soon as we get proof that Rex was the one who hurt you then your life can go back to normal." He stepped closer and feathered his fingertips across the lump on her temple.

"No, not back to normal," she contradicted. "Better than it was because now I have you back." She rested against his chest, and he wrapped his arms around her.

"Can't argue with that." His life was better now that he had Mia back and he wasn't letting Rex take her away from him. They'd find Lucy Barrow, he'd find something to nail Rex Stevens to the wall, and then he and Mia were free to restart their lives together.

\* \* \* \* \*

2:42 P.M.

"You're making me dizzy."

Mia stopped what she was doing and looked over at Poppy who was busily filing away paperwork. "I'm not doing anything, I'm just sitting here."

"You've been spinning that pen in your fingers for the last two hours. It keeps catching my attention out of the corner of my eye, it's driving me crazy, and it's making me dizzy," Poppy said, pausing to face her. "Look, I know this is rough, you want to be out there searching for Lucy Barrow, but it's safer for you here."

"I know," she said, setting the pen down on the table. Knowing she was safer here was one thing, but sitting idly around while her team searched for a missing child was a special kind of torture.

It was her job to rescue people.

Sitting here twiddling her thumbs—or spinning a pen between her fingers—felt like she was letting down both Lucy and her team.

"Just because it's the right thing to stay here doesn't mean I have to like it," she told Poppy.

"I know." Her friend smiled sympathetically. "It's always hard to be left out."

"Especially when it's your job." She checked the time for what felt like the hundredth time since Julian and the others had left to assist with the search. "I thought we would have heard something by now. What if he didn't just drug her this time and leave her where she would be found? What if he hurt her? What if he k-killed her?" Mia had to force the word out, she had no idea how she would cope if that cute little girl had died because of her.

Little Lucy Barrow was only six years old. She was missing her two front teeth, had the most adorable blonde curls, huge blue eyes, and a smattering of freckles across her cheeks. Lucy loved animals, and more than once Mia had found the little girl out in the woods tending to a baby bird, or lizard, or some other creature she had come across and decided to help.

Last time Mia had seen the child was about two weeks ago. Lucy had been at the supermarket with her mother and baby brother and had been stopping everyone to tell them that she was going to be dressing up as a panda bear for Halloween.

"What if he killed her, Poppy?" she whispered, distraught at the very notion.

"There's no reason to think that," Poppy said, coming over to wrap an arm around her shoulders. "Try not to get ahead of yourself. There's no reason to think that she won't be found safe and sound like the other children."

"Yeah, you're right," Mia said, forcing away all thoughts of the sweet child's lifeless corpse lying out in the middle of the forest for the birds and animals to eat if she wasn't found.

"Why don't you go make us some coffee," Poppy suggested. "I know I could use a cup and you look like you could too."

"Sure." It was better than sitting here and imagining every horrible thing her stalker could do to Lucy.

Taking her gun with her because she knew Julian would freak

if she didn't, she headed for the small kitchen. She was surprised that Julian had left her and Poppy here alone, she knew he was confident that Rex was her stalker, and that Rex would be at the search along with everyone else, but she hadn't expected him to be able to let her out of his sight for any reason.

Mia was crossing the foyer to the kitchen on the other side when she saw something resting against the door.

Automatically her feet changed direction, curious to see what it was, not really thinking anything of it.

It wasn't until she stood in front of the glass door that she realized what it was.

Flowers.

"You don't know they're for you," she whispered to herself.

Which was a lie.

Who else would they be for?

The police department didn't get random bouquets of flowers left on the doorstep.

Had Rex left them before he'd gone out to the search and rescue base? She and Poppy had gone straight through to the office when the others had left, so whoever had left them would have been able to walk right up to the door and no one would have seen him.

With trembling fingers, she had unlocked the door and picked up the flowers before she even realized what she was doing.

Julian would be mad.

She closed and locked the door and then she saw them.

The flowers.

They were dead.

A message?

"What is it?" Poppy demanded as she came running into the foyer.

How did her friend know about the flowers?

"Mia? What is it? Why did you scream?" Poppy—with her gun in her hand—was looking anxiously around.

Scream?

Did she scream?

She didn't remember making a sound, but Poppy was obviously here so she must have.

"S-someone left these," she said, holding out the bouquet. "They're dead."

"You have to call Julian," Poppy said, taking the bouquet from her arms.

Right.

Right.

Yes, she had to call Julian, tell him that her stalker had been here. No doubt if the precinct hadn't been locked then he would have walked right in. Last time he'd knocked her out and tried to kidnap her, this time she was sure he would have tried the same thing. And what would he have done to Poppy? Drugged her and left her here? Killed her?

Her hands were shaking so badly that when she retraced her steps to the office and picked up her phone it fell through her fingers, landing with a soft clunk on the carpeted floor.

Picking it up, Mia dropped down into a chair and dialed Julian. He answered on the first ring.

"Hey, honey, I was just about to call you with an update. We found Lucy Barrow, she's all right, drugged like the others and being transported to the hospital, but he didn't hurt her."

Relief stole her breath for a moment. She'd been so scared that the little girl might not survive, that her stalker would harm her just out of frustration that he hadn't been able to get his hands on her yet.

"Mia? You there?"

"Yes," she said quietly. "I'm glad about Lucy, but I wasn't calling for an update."

"What's wrong?" Julian asked, his perceptive cop brain already jumping to worst-case scenarios.

"Poppy and I are okay," she assured him, "but someone left

another bouquet of flowers just outside, leaning against the door."

"Rex showed up just a few minutes after we did. He had time to go to this car, then wait for us to leave before sneaking back to leave the flowers, and then drive out there."

"Julian, the flowers were … dead," she told him. She had no idea what that meant, but she didn't need to have a degree in criminal psychology to know it wasn't anything good.

"Is the door still locked?" he asked.

"Yes."

"You still have your gun?"

"Yes, I kept it with me just like I promised."

"I'm on my way back." His words were accompanied by the muffled sounds of him yelling to someone and then the clunk as a car door slammed.

"This feels different," she said, more to herself than to Julian.

"He's getting annoyed that he hasn't been able to get what he wants."

"He's escalating," she agreed. What did that mean for the children of River's End? She knew that she was safe with Julian, but despite their best efforts at warning parents not to let their children out alone, the stalker managed to keep finding victims. Would he start taking his frustrations out on them?

"He won't lay a hand on you," Julian vowed.

"It's not me that I'm worried about." If it came down to a choice, her or the innocent children of her town, she knew her decision.

"I know what you're thinking," Julian said, his voice harsh. "And you can just get those thoughts out of your pretty blonde head."

Mia rolled her eyes even though she knew that he couldn't see her. "I don't want anyone else hurt because some lunatic is obsessed with me."

"And I don't want you hurt."

Tears filled her eyes. She didn't want to be hurt, she didn't want to go through what she had with Joshua all over again, especially now, but she also didn't want anyone else hurt.

"Trust me, Mia. I know that I didn't save you last time, I know that you suffered unimaginable horrors because of it, but please, have faith in me. I will find the proof we need to arrest Rex, and if it turns out not to be him, then I will find whoever is terrorizing you. I will end this for you, Mia, I promise you that I will, but I need you to trust in me, believe in me."

His tone was so imploring, and she knew that he did indeed *need* her to believe in him. He'd suffered too, and she'd vowed not to make the same mistakes this time as she had last time, and that meant remembering that her being stalked impacted both of them, not just her.

Drawing in a deep breath, she calmed her racing heart. "Okay. I trust you, Julian, and I believe in you. I know that you will keep me safe."

# OCTOBER 12<sup>TH</sup>

8:28 A.M.

This was very annoying.

No.

Scratch that.

It was infuriating.

Mia Taylor was supposed to have paid for her sins already.

The woman was like Teflon, things just kept bouncing off her, and no matter what she did, she came out of it smelling like roses.

It wasn't fair.

And it wasn't going to last any longer.

That was a certainty you could take to the bank.

Snatching the children and leaving them out in the forest hadn't worked. Well, it almost had. Mia had been out there alone and had been ripe for the picking if not for that ridiculous guard dog of a husband. Ex-husband. No, estranged husband. Well, estranged husband turned un-estranged—non-estranged? No longer estranged?—whatever, it was clear that Mia and Julian Black were back together.

Of course everything always turned out perfect for Mia.

Just another reason to hate the woman.

Everyone thought she was so perfect, the whole town seemed to be in love with her, as far as they were concerned she could do no wrong.

Showed what they knew.

Mia wasn't the perfect little princess that everyone thought she was.

She had blood on her hands.

Lots of it.

And it was time that she finally paid for her sins.

Since luring her out in search of missing children—children who hadn't been harmed of course, there was no need to punish them for Mia's actions—hadn't yielded the desired results it was time to try something different.

Something bigger.

Mia hadn't participated in the last search, obviously her guard dog husband hadn't allowed it, but there was something that would get her running. The husband was starting to become a problem, interfering where he shouldn't be, getting between Mia and her destiny. If Julian Black didn't back off then he was going to have to be eliminated.

Permanently.

The minibus came along the road, and when the driver saw the car stopped in the middle of the road with the hood popped up they pulled to a stop unable to pass on the narrow country road.

Climbing out of the car—that was working perfectly fine and was merely a distraction—a wave at the bus had the driver opening the door.

"Car trouble?" the older man called out.

"Unfortunately, yes. And to make things worse my phone has died. Is there any chance at all I could borrow a phone to call for a tow?"

A middle-aged woman—a middle school science teacher who was taking the kids in the science club out on a school field trip to perform several experiments—smiled and rose from her seat as she rifled through her bag. "Here you go," she said as she handed over the latest iPhone.

Taking the phone and standing in the doorway, they made sure to remain inside the bus while faking a phone call and keeping a close watch.

"Okay, kids, I know this is a temporary delay in our day, but

SOME TRUST CAN BE REBUILT

while we wait for the tow truck to arrive I want you to go over your hypothesis and make sure you're ready to get working today," Mrs. Bucket instructed.

"Mrs. Bucket?" a tall skinny boy with thick red hair raised his hand.

"Yes, Kurt?"

"Do you really think our solar oven would be able to cook pizza?"

"Well," the teacher said thoughtfully, tucking a lock of her gray-streaked chestnut hair behind her ear. "I think that we probably don't have enough time to cook something that needs that much cooking, but it's a sunny day so I think we should definitely be able to cook our smores and maybe some nachos."

"I brought some potatoes, they're my favorite, I want to try baking some," a pretty brunette with hair that looked long enough to sit on announced to the bus.

The driver had turned in his seat to watch the kids, who all looked excited about the day's activities, and with everyone distracted it seemed like the perfect time to strike.

Strike like a snake.

Hidden in plain sight—camouflaged by small-town life that dulled the senses and made it so anyone you knew was seen as family and not a threat—hidden fangs were ready to take down the enemy in an efficient manner.

Surreptitiously the phone was dropped out of the bus—they wouldn't need it where they were going—and a gun was retrieved from the backpack. With a last look around to make sure everybody was otherwise occupied, it was time. Finally, time to make this happen.

"Everybody, throw your phones out the window."

The order made everybody stop talking and turn to look. When they saw the gun aimed at the bus driver's head fear crossed their faces. One girl screamed, another started crying, the teacher tried to move so she was in between the weapon and the children—pointless though that may be. No one was going to get shot, so long as they did as they were told. Hurting them wasn't part of the plan, they were a tool and nothing more, but if backed into a corner it could happen.

Still, that was just a last resort.

"I'm going to say it one more time, throw all your phones out of the bus." Phones were like a beacon calling in the darkness, leading anyone who was looking for the soon-to-be missing busload of kids straight to them.

"Please," Mrs. Bucket said, holding up her hands, palms out, to show that she wasn't a threat. "Please, don't hurt us. We'll do what you say, just please don't hurt anyone."

"No one will get hurt if you do as I say."

She nodded agreeably. "Kids, throw your phones out the window."

"But, Mrs. Bucket—"

"It's okay, Richie," Mrs. Bucket reassured the kid. "Just do as we're told and everything will be okay. Right?"

"Right. Now, you, move."

The bus driver looked like he was going to argue and try to play the hero, but all that would earn him was a bullet through the brain. Desperate times called for desperate measures, and Mia was going to pay once and for all. No way could even her guard dog of a husband stop her from searching for over a dozen kids along with their teacher and bus driver. As soon as she was out there, preferably alone, but whoever she was with would be eliminated, her life was over.

Cocking the gun was enough to have the driver getting with the program, and he stood and moved further back into the bus, putting himself in front of the teacher as a second line of defense for the children.

"Why don't you let the kids go," the older man said. "You'd still have me."

"And me," Mrs. Bucket added.

"So the kids aren't really necessary for whatever you have planned," the bus driver continued.

Actually, they were.

They were imperative in fact.

"The kids stay. Put these on everyone, hands behind their back." Unsure of how many kids were actually in the science club and thinking it was better to be over-prepared than under-prepared there were enough sets of plastic zip ties to cuff everyone on the bus with several left over.

The man hesitated, but a glance at the gun spurred him into action, and he took the zip ties and worked his way down one side of the bus and then up the other, cuffing the hands of each of the kids behind their back. It wasn't like the kids were much of a threat. The oldest couldn't be more than thirteen, but better safe than sorry.

"Her hands get cuffed to the back of the seat." The teacher had a look about her that said she would become a problem so it was better to take extra precautions with her. "Now you, I'm going to cuff to the steering wheel, I don't want you thinking you can play at being the hero."

The bus driver glared but didn't put up a fight, coming and sitting down, allowing himself to be cuffed to the steering wheel without doing anything stupid.

"I'll move the car and then I'll give you instructions. You follow them, and none of those kiddies get hurt, you try anything and I'll shoot one of them. Got it?"

"Got it," the driver grunted.

It was a relief once the car was moved and they were all on the bus. With everything under control, all the kids contained, and the bus driving off down the street, it had all gone so smoothly that it was almost hard to believe it. All they had to do now was drive to the chosen spot—a spot chosen to be hard to find and hard to extract the kidnapped kids and their keepers—and then all that was left to do was wait for Mia to come running into the trap.

She would.

She couldn't help herself.

The woman had a God complex a mile long.

She'd come running in, determined to be the one to save the children, the one to get the glory, so she could be worshipped by the stupid residents of River's End.

Soon they would see.

They would see that Mia was no hero.

They would all see the truth.

Mia was about to face the consequences of her actions.

\* \* \* \* \*

9:19 A.M.

"Why do you need a list of all the rescues I've done recently?" Mia asked. There were dark circles under her eyes, and Julian wished he could kiss them away, but they weren't at home they were at the station, and that meant he had to be at least marginally professional.

"We don't know for sure that Rex is your stalker, so we need to look into every avenue," he explained.

"What about the car angle? Didn't that go anywhere?" Mia asked. She sounded frustrated, and he tried not to take it personally since he knew that she wasn't annoyed with him, just the situation.

"Almost everyone in town who owns a car similar to the one seen at Rowan's attempted abduction has brought it in to be examined for evidence, so far we haven't found any. No cars have been brought in with a shot-out back tire, but Rex's car has disappeared, he's driving a rental."

"Further evidence that it's Rex who's been sending me flowers."

"And it probably is him, but we still have to look into other possibilities. There's a chance that it's a family member of someone who died, who you weren't able to find or rescue in time."

"There aren't many of those," Mia said. "Only a handful of losses over the last year."

"Start with those then. Any of them stand out in your memory?"

"No, not really." She shook her head slowly, looking thoughtful.

"Any relatives get angry with you? Maybe blame you for their loss?"

When he and Mia had been together, he could remember a few times where the grieving family had taken out their grief on Mia because she was a convenient target. He was sure there had to be a few more such instances over the eighteen months they had been apart.

"Maybe one or two," she replied.

"Either of them stand out?"

"There was one guy, it was last winter, he and his wife and young son were out skiing and they got lost. They stumbled upon one of the caves and he left them there while he continued on trying to find help. We found him first, but by the time we tracked down the cave his wife and little boy were already dead," Mia told him. "He was angry, said we should have found them faster. He said I had no business running search and rescue if I couldn't even perform a simple search. They'd wandered a long way, outside the search area where we thought they would be." She said the last like it was a personal failing on her part.

"You can't save everyone, Mia," Julian reminded her. "Did you do everything you could to find that family?"

She nodded.

"And I bet you stood there and let that man rant and rave at you without saying a word in your defense."

"He needed an outlet for his grief. But he went back home,

182

and I never heard from him again."

"I'll look into him. Do you remember his name?"

"Benson Wright," she answered without hesitation, and Julian wasn't surprised that she had remembered the man. Mia took everyone's pain onboard which was why it was so hard for her to deal with her own.

"I'll start with him, but I want you to write down every one of your losses because we will check all of them out."

Mia sighed. "Okay, I still think it's a waste of time, but ..."

She broke off as the door to the office he shared with the other River's End deputies was flung open and Beau stood there, a dark look on his face. Mia shuddered, and he wrapped an arm around her shoulders before asking, "Another missing kid?"

"Not just one," Beau replied.

"He took more than one?" Mia asked tightly.

Throwing her a quick sympathetic glance, Beau nodded. "The science club is missing. Sixteen middle school kids along with their teacher, Mrs. Bucket, and Simon Flanders who was driving the bus."

"And we think it's our guy?" Julian asked. It was quite a jump to go from relatively low-risk abductions of a single child to taking a whole bus full of people. This guy was either getting more confident or he was getting more desperate. Neither of those options meant anything good for the missing kids or for Mia.

"Best guess says it is unless we have someone else targeting kids in town," Beau replied.

"How do we know they're missing?" Julian asked.

"All of their phones were found discarded on the road next to an abandoned stolen car. Each of the phones had the same text message, it said 'You'll never find where he hid me'."

"He took them out into the forest," Mia said. "It's what he did with the kids. He left them out there because he wanted to lure me out into the forest to try to get me alone with no witnesses to see him grab me. That didn't work so he upped his game, he was probably annoyed that I wasn't part of the search yesterday and thought that if he wanted to get me involved he had to do something big."

"Well, unlucky for him his game won't work," Julian said. There was no way he was letting this guy get his hands on Mia. No way.

"Oh, yes it will," Mia shot back, giving him that determined look that told him convincing her otherwise wasn't going to be easy.

"I think that's my cue to leave." Beau gave them both a rueful smile before leaving the room.

"Mia, you know you can't go out there."

"I know no such thing." She surged to her feet, hands on her hips, and met his gaze squarely even though she had to crane her head back to do so.

"It's not safe."

"Those kids aren't safe."

"There are other people who can run this search."

"Maybe so, but I *will* be part of it. I'm not sitting around the police station, all safe and sound, while over a dozen innocent kids are scared out of their minds, possibly hurt, maybe even close to death." Her cheeks, which had been pale from lack of sleep and the toll dealing with a second stalker was taking on her, were now stained pink with outrage.

He got it.

He did.

Knowing that someone was hurting other people to get to her was the worst kind of hell, but this was about logic and reason not about emotion.

"You're not going." He didn't want to sound like a jerk, but it was what it was. It was his job to protect her, and there was no way he was letting her walk into a trap.

"Oh?" Mia arched a disbelieving brow. "So you're the boss of me now?"

"When it comes to your safety, absolutely."

Mia looked about ready to explode. She stabbed a finger into his chest and her green eyes were all but spitting fire at him. "Look, mister, just because we're back together does not mean you get to tell me what I can and can't do. You think I'm some sort of idiot? I know that it's dangerous to go and join in the search, and I don't expect to go alone. I thought your stupid self would come with me. That way I wouldn't be alone, and I can still do my job and help find those kids before one of them dies. How do you expect me to live with myself if that happens? Did you think of that, huh?"

He had thought of it.

And he knew it would crush her.

So it looked like he had a choice. He could lock Mia away and refuse to let her put herself in any sort of danger and then watch her die a slow death from guilt over others being hurt on her behalf. Or he could go with her, watch her back, and try to accept that Mia was built a lot like him, the need to protect ran deep in both of their souls.

Julian sighed, he knew what he had to do.

Dragging Mia into his arms, he tightened his hold when she struggled against him. "Okay."

"Okay?" she asked, going still and looking up at him. "I can go?"

"You don't leave my sight for a second, not for any reason at all."

"I wasn't planning to."

"I mean it, Mia. You stick to me like glue. No running off because one of the kids is in trouble, no taking any risks at all no matter how small. We go, we take a grid in the search area, and we search it together," he said, laying down the ground rules.

"Fine, no arguments from me." She wrapped her arms around his waist and kissed his jaw. "Thank you for understanding that this is something I have to do."

"I don't like it," he warned.

"I know, but you're forgetting something."

"What?"

"I trust you. You're trained for this, to protect people, and I know without a shadow of a doubt that you will keep me safe."

The seriousness in her face struck him deep, and he knew he would do anything, including give his own life, to keep Mia safe.

\* \* \* \* \*

10:40 A.M.

"I don't like this."

Mia rolled her eyes at Julian's back as they walked through the forest, he wouldn't see her, but it made her feel better. "I know, you've told me at least a hundred times in the last hour."

"There are sixty minutes in an hour, and sixty seconds in a minute, so three thousand six hundred seconds in an hour, I figure it takes three seconds to say 'I don't like this', so the maximum number of times I could say it would be one thousand two hundred. If I said it one hundred times in that time that would mean I was saying it every twelve seconds. I think that's highly unlikely."

"You're really obnoxious sometimes, you know that?" Mia glared at Julian's back. "And you're such a math geek."

"It's not my fault you're no good at it."

"I remember in ninth grade when I was failing geometry, and you refused to help me."

"Help you cheat was what you wanted me to do. Cheating on tests doesn't help you learn anything."

"You were always such a goody-two-shoes," she muttered under her breath.

"You're one to talk, you were the teacher's pet since first grade," Julian muttered back.

"I was never a teacher's pet," she shot back.

"You were, and you know it."

"You're impossible." Had Julian been this annoying when they were together last time? She knew that he was worried about her and that he didn't want to be out here with her. She should cut him a break, he *had* agreed to let her come out here to help search because he knew it was important to her.

"Remember when you used to bring an apple to the teacher every day in the third grade." Julian laughed. "Remember that time when you were late to school because you just had to get Mrs. Hinkle the biggest apple you could find so you climbed the tree in the Noonan's front yard? You climbed up and got your apple, but you slipped coming down and landed in that huge puddle. It had been raining for days and you were covered in mud, and you didn't want to be seen all messed up so you had to sneak back home and change." Julian laughed again like it was the funniest thing that had ever happened.

Mia scowled but had to fight to keep her lips from curving into a smile. She did remember that day, she'd been so determined that she would bring an apple for Mrs. Hinkle every single day, but when she'd fallen into that puddle she'd been too embarrassed to let the teacher see her. "My dad caught me as I tried to sneak back inside. He marched me down to the school all covered in mud to explain to Mrs. Hinkle why I was late. I was so mad at him I wouldn't talk to him for a week." She smiled now at the memory, but the smile turned sad because she knew that there would never be moments like the ones she had shared with her dad between him and her children.

Julian stopped and closed the short distance between them, all traces of teasing or irritation gone, his hands clasped her upper arms, and he leaned down so they were eye to eye. "He wouldn't want you to get sad when you think of him."

"He's going to be gone soon." They would find who was stalking her, there was an end in sight even if it didn't feel like it, but with her dad the end was him being gone forever.

"And when he is gone, he'd want you to smile when you think of him, to laugh when you reminisce, to only remember the good times not the bad."

"I don't know how to do that," she whispered as tears blurred her vision.

"Then I'll help you." His arms came around her, drawing her into an embrace, and the small circles he rubbed on her back went a little way toward soothing her.

"I'm going to miss him so much," she murmured into Julian's chest.

"Yeah, you will."

"He's going to miss out on so much. He won't get to see me have kids or get to hold them and make them laugh with his silly jokes, and he won't be there when they learn to walk and go to school. I won't get to see him grow old. Every time I see him I wonder if it will be the last ... I can't let him go, I don't want to."

Julian just tightened his hold on her, and she curled her hands into his sweater and clung to him. It was so unfair, she'd lost her mother before she ever even got to know her and she and her dad had been a team ever since. Now he was dying, and she could already not stand the pain of losing him, and he wasn't even gone yet. How would she cope when it actually happened?

As though reading her mind, Julian kissed the top of her head before saying, "Together. We'll cope with it together."

"I'm so glad I have you back." Her arms moved to wrap around Julian's waist and she breathed in his scent. There was no way she could have dealt with her dad's impending death alone, but together she just might be able to make it through.

She pulled herself together, now wasn't the time to be wallowing in her own problems, there were sixteen kids and their teacher and bus driver out there somewhere and they needed her to be focused. She could do this, she had begged to be able to be out here doing this, so it was time to get her mind back on track.

Easing out of Julian's arms, she immediately missed his warmth and the comfort of his touch, but she fortified her spine and shoved her mind back into work mode. There would be plenty of time for her to fall apart later, and Julian was right, her dad wouldn't want her to miss him and be sad. He'd want her to focus on all the good times they had shared and remember that he would always be with her in her heart.

"Julian, I was thinking about where he might leave the kids."

"And you have an idea?"

"Maybe. He took them in the bus, and if he truly doesn't want to hurt them, he probably left them in there. He can't just drive the bus into the forest and leave it there, too easy to be found, and he needs to make sure I'm out here before that happens. So I was thinking where I would hide a bus, and there's this place, it's just at the base of the mountain where there's this rocky outcrop, it would be a tight fit, but you could get the bus underneath. It would be hard to spot, and if he wanted to, he might be able to board up the entrance a little."

"Sounds like a place—" Julian broke off abruptly as a crack split through the air.

A moment later, red bloomed on his chest, and he was reaching for his gun even as he dropped to the ground.

He wasn't moving.

Was he dead?

Mia felt like she left her body, panic and fear over Julian left her frozen, even as she knew she had to do something, pull out her own weapon, run to Julian, do something ... anything ... but she didn't, she just stood there in shock staring at the lifeless body of the man she loved.

Another crack had her snapping out of her stupor as a bullet flew by, embedding in the trunk of the tree a foot to her right sending bits of bark spitting everywhere.

A sting in her cheek washed away the last of the cobwebs and she ran to Julian, throwing her body over his.

Any hope that this might be some sort of weird accident was dashed when another bullet hit the ground, this time in front of them, and sticks and dirt flew into her face.

They were being shot at.

It had to be her stalker.

This was all her fault, Julian hadn't wanted to come out here, hadn't thought it was safe, but she had been sure that as long as he was by her side then she would be okay.

Now he might be dead because of her.

A figure dressed all in black came running toward her and Mia fumbled with the gun Julian had insisted she carry.

She managed to pry it free, but their attacker was almost on her. Praying that since she was the target their focus would be on her not Julian, she rolled to the side, lying on her back.

Just as she managed to aim the gun at the man in black, he swung something at her and pain exploded inside her skull.

She fired.

Over and over again.

Until the darkness claimed her and she faded away into nothingness.

\* \* \* \* \*

1:23 P.M.

Pain hammered a steady beat in his head.

The same pain was echoed in his chest.

But something hurt deeper down, a fear that he couldn't quite comprehend, but he knew without a shadow of a doubt that something was drastically wrong.

Julian slowly became more aware of his surroundings. Hushed voices spoke, something beeped a steady rhythm, and something scratchy covered his bare chest.

Bare chest?

With a groan, Julian opened his eyes and forced his usually focused mind to snap to attention. It took longer than it should have and it wasn't until Abe and his brother Will noticed he was awake and crossed to stand beside him that it finally dawned on him where he was.

The hospital.

Just like that, everything fell into place.

The busload of missing kids, Mia's insistence that she take part in the search, his bad feeling that he was putting her in harm's way, the gunshot, the pain, then nothing.

Until now.

"Where's Mia?" he demanded, irritated when his voice came out weak and scratchy. He didn't have time for that now.

"You need to stop moving about," Will said, placing a hand on his shoulder and trying to force him to relax against the mattress.

That wasn't going to happen.

He didn't need the details to know that something was wrong.

If he'd been shot and Mia was able she would be sitting here beside his bed waiting for him to wake up.

Unless she'd been hurt too.

Or worse.

As he saw it there were only two options. Mia was either somewhere here in the hospital or the stalker had gotten what he wanted and Mia was lost, possibly forever.

"Where. Is. Mia?" he asked, punctuating each word.

Will and Abe exchanged glances. They wanted to try to keep the truth from him, probably because they thought they were doing what was best for him, but they didn't understand that there was nothing worse than not knowing what was going. He didn't want to be kept in the dark no matter how bad things were.

"Tell me," he demanded.

Will sighed then said, "By the time we found you she was gone."

The bottom fell out of his world.

"Gone?"

How could she just be gone?

They'd been bickering, him annoyed that he'd given in and let her put herself in danger, and her because he wouldn't let her forget it, then they'd talked about her dad, he'd held her, comforted her. How could in the very next moment she have disappeared?

"What happened?" he asked.

"We were hoping you would be telling us that," Abe said.

"Someone shot at us. The first shot hit me and took me out." He didn't bother to ask what it had hit and how badly he was hurt, he could talk, he could think, he could move, that was all that mattered. "What did you find at the scene?"

Another exchanged glance between his brother and his cousin. "There was some blood," Abe said.

"Some blood?" What did that mean? He took it that it was in addition to his own blood so obviously Mia's since she had gone missing, but was it enough blood to indicate that she was probably still alive or enough that said she was probably already gone?

"It wasn't enough that we think she's dead," Will assured him.

"But she is hurt," he said, and while he was relieved she was alive she was far from okay.

"Anything else? Evidence? Something?" Frustration seeped into each word. He was so tired of always being one—or ten— steps behind this guy. They needed to get ahead of him if they wanted even a chance at getting Mia back alive.

"We didn't find anything at the scene, just you with a bullet wound in your chest—since you haven't asked, you were lucky, the bullet deflected off your ribs instead of piercing your heart or your lungs—and a puddle of blood about five feet from you," Will told him.

While he was glad the bullet hadn't hit a lung or his heart because if it had he would be out of commission and unable to help in the search for Mia, he hadn't asked because he didn't care about his injury. "The kids?"

"Someone—we're assuming Mia's stalker—called in the location of the bus, I presume after he got his hands on her. That's how we realized something was wrong. You and Mia didn't check in when the call came through that the kids and teacher had all been found and were unharmed, so we went looking for you," Abe explained.

"So we were right, they were another distraction, a way to lure Mia into a trap and it worked. This time he obviously wasn't going to let anything stop him from getting her." And he had no one to blame but himself for the stalker getting what he wanted.

He'd known better than to let her go out there.

He should have locked her in a cell at the station if that was what it took to stop her.

Now she was gone and it might be too late.

"What did the teacher and kids say? Did they identify their abductor?" he asked.

"They're all still asleep, they were drugged like the others," Abe replied.

"Where was Rex during the search?" he asked.

Abe and Will glanced at each other, a silent conversation passing between them as they obviously decided how much to tell him.

He wasn't in the mood for games.

This was his wife they were talking about—his very heart—and he wanted in on everything.

"Tell me," he ordered.

"Rex Stevens is dead," Abe said.

"Dead?" he echoed, his heart dropping. Rex was their only suspect, with him dead that left them standing in the middle of a haystack searching for that proverbial needle.

"Best guess is at least twelve hours ago," Will told him. "He was stashed in his basement. We found his car, it didn't have a tire shot out."

Further proof that Rex wasn't Mia's stalker.

"There was a man Mia was telling me about this morning, from a rescue last winter. He and his family got lost, his wife and son didn't make it, Mia said he blamed her, was pretty angry with her about it." They had to look into this man and then everyone else connected to anyone Mia hadn't been able to save. The stalker was out there somewhere, and there had to be a link. All they had to do was keep looking and they'd find it.

"I don't think it's him," Abe said.

"How can you know that?"

"Rex was found naked from the waist down, and someone had stabbed him in the groin, almost severed his … uh … thing," Will finished with a wince.

He and Abe winced along with him. No guy wanted to think about that. "So, what? You think that Rex was killed by a woman?"

"It would make sense. Looks like he was killed in the bedroom, blood on the bed and his clothes on the floor beside it," Abe said.

"So then this woman who pretends she wants to sleep with him kills him and then drags him down to the basement? Rex isn't a small guy." Julian wasn't sure he was on board with this theory.

"No, he's not," Abe agreed. "But someone with training on how to move people much larger than themselves could do it."

"I guess," he agreed. "It would have to be someone trained in something like …" he trailed off as he realized what he'd been about to say. His eyes met the others. "It would have to be someone with training like search and rescue. Are we looking for a woman on the search and rescue team?"

"That's our working theory," Will confirmed.

"There's only one other woman on the search and rescue team."

Abe nodded. "Eileen Glass."

"But why would Eileen want to hurt Mia? She's only lived here a few months and Mia considers her a friend."

"Doesn't mean Eileen feels the same way," Abe reminded him.

"I know that, but a woman stalking another woman, that's not common, and stalkers always have a reason for why they get obsessed with someone. What's Eileen's reason?"

"We could ask her, but she never came back after the search," Will said.

"We have to find her, we have to find out why she's obsessed with Mia." Julian threw back the thin, scratchy hospital blankets and swung his legs over the side of the bed, ignoring the pain in his chest that felt like someone had shoved a dozen knives in there.

"I don't think you're being discharged yet," Abe said.

Julian just glowered. There was no way he was sitting around in a bed while Mia was out there at the hands of someone who wanted to destroy her.

No way.

He was going to find Mia, and he was going to pray that she could forgive him for failing her a second time.

One thing was sure, he would never forgive himself.

Thanks to him, Mia was fighting for her life again, and this time she might not survive.

\* \* \* \* \*

3:04 P.M.

Mia came alert with a start.

Disorientation made it hard to figure out exactly where she was and what had happened to make her feel so awful.

Her head hurt.

Her arm throbbed.

An image of a figure in black running toward her sent fear

cutting through her.

Julian.

He'd been shot.

She remembered the blood on his clothing and the way he lay so still beneath her as she did her best to protect him from the flying bullets.

Had it been pointless?

Was he already dead?

No.

He couldn't be.

He wouldn't do that to her.

He wouldn't walk back into her life only to get himself killed and leave her all over again.

Only he might not have had a choice.

Logically, she knew that. Julian would have fought with everything he had not to leave her, but the bullet may have made the decision for him.

What had happened to him?

What had happened to her?

Mia tried to take in her surroundings, but she was woozy and sleepy and all she wanted to do was drift away into whatever quiet, peaceful zone she had just emerged from.

But she couldn't.

She had to know where she was.

She tried to move, realized she couldn't, and panic had her jerking violently against her bonds. The resulting pain was enough to have her plunging back into unconsciousness whether she liked it or not.

Darkness blanketed her.

Then all of a sudden unbearable pain had her screaming as she was torn from sleep.

"Enough, I'm tired of waiting for you to wake up, I gave you the correct dosage for your size, you should have woken up already," a faraway voice ranted.

The voice was familiar, but she couldn't seem to place it.

Her entire world had morphed into nothing but pain.

"Come on." The words were accompanied by searing agony in one of her arms, and Mia groaned, panting, as her eyes flickered open.

As soon as they did her stomach dropped.

She knew this room.

She had suffered in this room before.

Almost lost her life in it.

But why was she back here?

This didn't make sense.

Unless ...

No.

Julian told her that Joshua Graves was indeed dead and that he hadn't come back to haunt her.

At least not in the normal sense.

But someone had brought her here to the same abandoned cabin where Joshua had intended to keep her locked up until he made her fall in love with him.

Why?

This didn't make sense.

None of it, the stalker, the missing kids, Julian being shot, her being back here, she didn't understand. The pounding in her head didn't help.

"So, are you awake or not?"

The snapped question had her gaze moving from the one-room cabin—which looked exactly as it had the last time she had been here only dirtier—to the speaker, and her mouth fell open in shock.

No.

It couldn't be.

Why did this just keep getting worse and worse?

"Eileen?" she asked or croaked in a weak voice that told her she wasn't going to be fighting her way out of here any time soon.

"What are you doing here?"

As far as she knew, Eileen didn't have a clue about this cabin, her friend—at least she'd thought they were friends—knew about her stalker, they'd talked about it a few times, but she'd never gone into details like giving directions to the cabin.

"Making you pay," Eileen said with a sneer. The woman standing before her looked nothing like the woman she had gotten to know over the last year. Gone were the bright, sparkling eyes and the warm, caring smile. In their place were eyes that were filled with anger and hatred, and a snarl that said bad things were coming.

"Making me pay?" she echoed. What did that mean? As far as she knew they'd been colleagues and friends who had enjoyed spending time together. What had she done to make Eileen hate her like this?

The more she woke up from her head injury meets drugged hangover, the more she realized that it wasn't just her head but her whole body that was hurting. The throbbing in her arm was from a bullet wound, and there was rope tied tightly around her wrists and ankles binding her to the bed.

The same bed where Joshua had raped her.

Panic beat a steady drum in her heart and tears leaked from her eyes.

What was she going to do?

How was she going to get out of here?

If she had learned anything from what happened with Joshua, it was that no matter how hard Julian looked for her, he might not find her. If she wanted to survive, then she had to rely on herself and herself alone.

Only problem was, she was injured this time.

She'd gotten shot when she fought Joshua for the gun last time, but before that she hadn't been physically assaulted which was how she'd managed to get her hands on the gun in the first place. This time she was shot before she even got here. She didn't like her chances of forming any sort of successful defense.

"You're not even listening." Eileen slapped her hard enough to make her head snap painfully to the side, making it pound like it had been ripped in half. "Why did you ask the question if you aren't even going to bother to listen to the answer?"

Lesson learned.

Eileen wanted attention and was going to throw a tantrum if she didn't get it.

"I'm sorry, my head hurts, it's hard to concentrate, I think I have a concussion, and I lost a lot of blood when the bullet hit my arm, I need to go to the hospital," she said, still clinging to some measure of denial and hoping Eileen would come to her senses.

"It's always about you, isn't it, Mia?" Eileen sneered. "Always about what you want, about what you need. Well, what about what I want?"

"What do you want, Eileen?"

"I want you to suffer, I want you to bleed, I want you to scream in pain and beg me to end your life. I want you to feel every ounce of pain that you made me feel."

"That I made you feel?"

"When you stole Joshua away from me," Eileen explained.

"Stole Joshua?" What on earth did Eileen mean by that?

"You already had a husband, but that wasn't enough for you, was it? You had to go after my man too."

"I didn't go after Joshua. He was stalking me, he kidnapped me, raped me, he nearly killed me."

"After he met you, all he could talk about was you. How beautiful you were, how sweet, how brave risking your life to save other people, but you know what? You haven't done anything that I couldn't do. I joined search and rescue, I saved lives, I'm just as pretty as you are, and I bet I'm better in bed than you are." The last was said with a wicked smile as Eileen pressed the tip of a knife to one of her breasts.

Her bare breast.

After shooting her, knocking her unconscious, and drugging her, Eileen must have brought her here then stripped off her clothes before tying her to the bed.

Great, that was just what she needed. She hated being this vulnerable to Eileen, unable to protect herself.

"Does Julian like these breasts?" Eileen asked as she ran the tip of the knife around her areola. "Does he like to touch them? Does he take your nipple into his mouth and suck on it?"

Eileen didn't seem to actually require an answer so Mia thought it was best to keep her mouth shut rather than risk provoking her.

"What about if I did this?" Eileen asked as she slashed the knife viciously across her breast making Mia grunt in pain. Blood flowed freely from the wound, but Eileen wasn't done. She slashed again and again until cuts crisscrossed her left breast.

The more Mia tried to move away from the knife the more the ropes tore at her wrists and ankles until they were slick with her blood.

"If Julian could see you now, I don't think he'd find you very pretty, would he?" Eileen asked, cocking her head to the side and studying her handiwork. "I cut myself you know, after I lost the only man I'd ever loved." She pulled up the sleeve of her sweatshirt to show a row of small scars running parallel to one another between her wrist and her elbow. "Every time I cut myself I thought of you. Of how it would feel to make you bleed." Eileen leaned in close to whisper in her ear, "Only now I don't have to imagine." Then she threw back her head and laughed.

Mia knew begging wouldn't work, and neither would logic. There was no way she was fighting her way out of this and no way she was talking her way out. If by some miracle she survived, all Julian would get back was a patchwork quilt of a woman who had lost the ability to fight.

"Wouldn't want this poor breast to feel left out."

As Eileen went to work marring her right breast, Mia let the pain knock her over into blissful unconsciousness.

\* \* \* \* \*

3:36 P.M.

Blood ran in dozens of rivulets down Mia's breast, puddling on the mattress beneath her.

Eileen had always been terrified of the sight of blood, and she'd actually passed out once in middle school when a softball hit her right in the nose, breaking it and giving her a bloody nose. When she'd seen the bright red sticky substance staining her hand she'd freaked out, started screaming hysterically before fainting dead away.

Middle school was a tricky time, stuck between childhood and adolescence, a time when you were finding yourself, learning who you were. A time where your peers could be particularly vicious.

As hers had been.

She'd been teased mercilessly for months afterward, isolating her even further and she withdrew into herself. Eileen had always been the quiet kid, the nerdy kid who didn't have a lot of friends and was always studying in the library. Only she wasn't in the library studying because she found it fun, she was there because she didn't have any friends and it filled the lonely hours at school.

Then she'd met Joshua, and her life had changed.

He was her everything.

Smart, hot, funny, he made her heart turn somersaults and her stomach flutter. She still remembered with crystal clear clarity the day she had met him. She'd graduated college with a degree in accounting and was ready to start looking for a job. Making a list of all of the firms in her city, she started visiting them in person. When she'd walked into Joshua's office to see if he had any job openings, it was love at first sight.

From her perspective anyway.

While he had offered her a job, he hadn't reciprocated her feelings.

They'd been friends, they'd go to the movies together, or out to dinner, they'd even gone on a vacation together one summer. She'd had all these plans about how she would sneak into his hotel room and seduce him, but when she'd cracked open his door, she'd heard him in bed with another woman.

Then he'd met Mia.

He'd driven through River's End on the way back from visiting his mother and seen her in the town's diner when he'd stopped for lunch. He'd been immediately smitten and when he'd returned all he'd talked about was how beautiful Mia was, how smart, how funny, how brave for risking her life working search and rescue. In the end, he had decided he couldn't live so far away from her and moved down there to the quaint little town.

She'd lost him.

The only friend she'd ever had.

Joshua had known that her family consisted of an alcoholic father—who at least was a pleasant drunk—a narcissistic mother, a sister who was the golden child, and a brother who was the beloved baby of the family, and yet he'd left her anyway.

And all for this pathetic woman whose bloody body lay tied helplessly to a bed.

Mia was the reason she had lost Joshua.

She had cast some sort of sex spell over him and stolen any chance Eileen had of winning his heart.

Then Mia had taken his life.

She had killed the man Eileen loved.

Killed him before Eileen could make him her own.

Now Mia had to pay for that.

The whole town thought she was so perfect, but Mia had had it easy, plenty of friends, a loving family, a man of her own, everything Eileen hadn't had.

Now she was going to destroy the woman, slice her to shreds but not kill her.

No, she wasn't going to end Mia's life. She was just going to make sure the woman was forced to live in pain and alone for the rest of her days.

Like Eileen had to.

No way would Julian Black want this scarred, pathetic version of Mia, he would dump her. She would be ugly, no longer sexy, and no longer able to do her job.

She would have nothing but the tattered remains of her scarred body and soul.

Maybe then Eileen would find some peace.

She had found peace in the flowing of her blood after she lost Joshua, and now she would find peace in the flowing of Mia's blood. Soothed by the very thing that used to terrify her because what was fear when you had already lost your heart? As Mia had shot Joshua, leaving him to bleed to death, so she had embraced the life essence of blood.

Mia had passed out when Eileen had started slicing up her right breast, and not wanting the woman to miss out on even a second of the pain she deserved, she'd stopped. Now she was ready to start again, she wanted to vent her anger, get her revenge, and then she wanted to live out Joshua's legacy.

She knew the way to do it too.

Eileen knew a secret about Joshua that not even his family had. Only she and Mia knew, and Mia certainly wouldn't be taking advantage of it.

"Wake up," she said loudly, slapping Mia's cheek.

Mia groaned, her eyelashes fluttering before her eyes slowly opened. "Eileen, please, don't do this. I never loved Joshua, he was just stalking me."

Eileen scoffed. "You had sex with him in this very bed," she said.

"He raped me."

203

"Pfft." As far as she was concerned that was semantics.

"How did you know about the cabin?"

"I read it in your diary," Eileen sneered. It had all been so easy, move to River's End, get a job at search and rescue to prove she was just as brave as Mia, and befriend her by pretending to be bubbly and outgoing. One night when they'd had a girl's night at Mia's, she'd waited till the woman had fallen asleep then gone snooping. The diary hadn't even been hidden away and as she read it, her hatred for Mia grew.

"If you read my diary then you know that nothing he did to me was my choice," Mia said.

"Excuses, excuses." She wasn't here to listen to Mia try to defend herself, she knew the facts. While Eileen had been trying to show Joshua how much she loved and adored him, he'd been fawning all over Mia.

Mia had to pay for that.

Without her interference, Eileen would have finally had the love and devotion she had always craved.

"Joshua was mine," she said, slashing the knife across Mia's chest, thrilled when the other woman gasped. "You stole him." Another swipe and she watched as blood bloomed from each gash, bright and bubbly.

That was who she had become.

Bright.

Bubbly.

Lethal.

Gone was the meek girl who was too afraid of her mother to step out of line, who was too insecure and unsure of herself to make friends, who had never had a boyfriend.

Now she was strong.

Powerful.

Confident.

She took control of every situation she faced and found a way to get the advantage.

"You know, we didn't quite finish what we started before since you decided to take a little nap," she said with a wide smile. The mixture of fear and pain in Mia's eyes stirred something inside her, a feeling deep in her belly that she had never felt before.

Was this what it felt like to be turned on?

She'd been attracted to Joshua, daydreamed about what it would be like to make love to him, but she had never felt this sensation before.

Was it the blood or Mia's suffering making her feel this way?

"Let's make this breast all matchy, matchy," she sing-songed, and she gave the right breast the same treatment she had given the left.

Tears trailed down Mia's cheeks, although she didn't cry out loud, the soft moans the escaped only served to further the heat pooling between her legs.

"I'm going to have his baby," she whispered. Too bad she couldn't get pregnant the conventional way, but still, having Joshua's baby growing inside her was what mattered.

That way he would be part of her forever.

"He collected his sperm, apparently there is such a thing as mail-in sperm freezing kits, you send them your stuff and they store it for you. He was going to use it on you but now it's mine," she hissed, her anger at the other woman flaring.

Mia had tried to steal Joshua, but in the end she would be the one to carry on his name.

She was the one whose love for Joshua was pure.

"You stole so much from me, Mia. I won't get to hear Joshua tell me he loves me, I won't get to make love to him or marry him, but I'm going to make sure that you lose everything too. Julian won't want you when I'm through with you, neither will your job or your friends. It will just be you, alone, forever."

Eileen knelt between the woman's legs and let the tip of the knife trail lightly up the inside of Mia's thigh.

"Does Julian like to touch you here? Does he kiss his way up your legs before putting his mouth on you? Let's see if we can change your memories. Now when you think of this you'll remember the feel of my knife slicing through your skin and not his lips."

* * * * *

4:04 P.M.

"Does Julian like to touch you here? Does he kiss his way up your legs before putting his mouth on you? Let's see if we can change your memories. Now when you think of this you'll remember the feel of my knife slicing through your skin and not his lips."

The words, said by a psychotic and highly unstable stalker who currently had Mia restrained did more damage to him than any bullet ever could.

How badly had Eileen Glass already hurt Mia?

It killed him that they didn't have eyes on her yet, but after looking into Eileen's past and learning that she had worked with Joshua before he'd moved to River's End, they had jumped to the logical conclusion that Eileen had been obsessed with Joshua and transferred that obsession to Mia who she blamed for his death. They had no idea how Eileen had learned so many details like the flowers and what order Joshua had sent them, but obviously she had learned those facts so they had assumed that she also knew about the cabin.

Making it the first place they had come to look for Mia.

Right now, he, Will, Abe, Sydney, Fletcher, and Beau, were all approaching the cabin as they heard Eileen's shrill voice taunting Mia.

Fury burned brightly inside him.

Bright enough that it dulled the pain in his chest every time he took a breath. It wasn't the first time he had broken a rib and it probably wouldn't be the last, but the timing really sucked. Mia needed him, and he wasn't at one hundred percent. Still, he wasn't sitting this out, if he could stand then he could be here, and he'd already argued until he was hoarse to convince Abe to let him come.

In the end, he was pretty sure it was only pity that Julian was begging that had convinced his cousin to agree, but Julian didn't care, so long as he was here, could hold her when they rescued her, that was all that mattered.

She was all that mattered.

Just as he approached one of the front windows, he heard Mia's pained moan and knew that Eileen's knife had made contact with her flesh.

Eileen Glass was a dead woman.

He wanted to take his knife—or hers—and slice her up just like she was doing to Mia, make her pay for terrorizing the woman he loved, opening old wounds and inflicting new ones.

Looking through the grimy window, Julian could see Mia tied spreadeagled to a bed, and the blood ...

It was everywhere.

It coated her chest, and her arms, rivulets of it streaked down her stomach and her sides and was soaked into the mattress she lay on.

He saw red.

If his brother hadn't grabbed hold of him, physically restrained him, he would have stormed in there with no thought to anything other than stopping this psychopath from hurting Mia.

"You go in there like that and you'll get her killed," Will murmured close to his ear. "I know this is Hell, believe me, but we do this the right way so we all walk out of this alive. Sydney is staying at the east window, and Beau at the west, Fletcher will take the south window leaving you and me and Abe to go in through the front door. Can you do that? I don't mean are you physically capable of it because I already know you're not, but are you going to be able to hold it together? Because if you can't, back out now. Mia's life is at stake."

Dragging in a long, slow breath, he relished the pain from his cracked rib, it gave him something to focus on besides the overwhelming terror.

Will was right.

He had to pull it together.

If he didn't, it would be Mia that paid the price.

Again.

He wasn't letting that happen.

"I'm good," he said.

Will nodded, then while the others took up position at the windows, their weapons trained on Eileen, he and Will and Abe moved to the front door.

Weapons drawn, as soon as they stormed through the door Eileen's attention snapped their way. She knelt on the bed, between Mia's spread legs, a knife in her hand, fresh blood dripping down the inside of Mia's leg.

Her eyes grew wide as she took in the three armed men staring her down, and Julian could practically see the wheels in her head turning.

Instead of turning the knife on Mia—as he had suspected she would do—Eileen turned it on herself, holding it to her neck. "You come any closer and I'll kill myself," she threatened.

As far as Julian was concerned Eileen could have at it, the world would be a better place without her in it, and he would love Mia to have the peace of mind of knowing her stalker was no longer alive and a potential threat. But that wasn't how this worked. They had a duty as officers of the law to do everything in their power to make sure everyone—including Eileen—walked out of this cabin alive.

"It's over, Eileen," he said with more calm than he felt. "We know you're the one who kidnapped and drugged all those children. There's no way you're walking away from this."

"It's over all right," Eileen sneered. "Your precious little Mia isn't so perfect anymore. I cut her up real good." Pride emanated from her and Julian seethed.

"Put the knife down, Eileen," he ordered. Mia lay limply on the bed, her eyes closed, she needed a hospital, and he was determined to get her there as quickly as possible. He wasn't standing around convincing Eileen to surrender, she would either put down her knife or he'd shoot her.

"I don't think so," Eileen said with a giggle. "You're not going to shoot me, and even if you did it wouldn't change anything. Mia will still be ruined, broken, destroyed, every time she looks at herself she'll remember me, and you won't even be able to stand the look of her. That makes me immortal. Even if you kill me I'll live on in your mind and Mia's, and everyone else in this town."

The woman was insane, there was no reasoning with someone who was this unbalanced. The hand that held the knife to her neck was steady, and Julian was sure she wouldn't hesitate to slice her neck if she deemed it her best option.

Just as he was about to instruct one of the others to take the shot and take her out, Mia suddenly jerked her hips off the bed, knocking Eileen off balance and sending her tumbling off the bed.

That was all they needed.

Abe ran to Eileen, kicking the knife away from her and pushing her into the floor as he pulled out handcuffs.

Not caring in the least about Eileen, Julian braced an arm around his aching ribs and ran to Mia's side. She was breathing hard, and tears were trailing down her cheeks, but she wasn't making a sound. Shoving his gun away he pulled out his knife. "Hold, on baby, I'll get you free in a moment."

Mia lay still and quiet, and he didn't like the way she kept her face turned away from him. Was she just hurting or did she believe that garbage Eileen had been spewing?

He prayed it was the former.

"Mia-bug, look at me, baby," he ordered as he sawed at the rope circling her wrists.

With a shuddering sigh, she finally tilted her head in his direction, and he let out a small breath.

She startled when Fletcher came toward them, and he put his lips against her ear and whispered, "It's okay, sweetheart, it's only Fletch."

"Just going to cut you free, honey," Fletcher said soothingly as he used his knife to saw through the rope attaching her ankles to the bed.

It didn't take them long, and Mia gasped and cried out as they got her free and blood circulation returned. Julian felt her pain as though it was his own, and when Fletcher reached to pick up Mia he shook his head and scooped her up and into his arms. His cracked rib screamed in protest at the added weight, but he ignored it. Mia was alive and in his arms and that was all that mattered. Carrying might not be good for his ribs, but he wasn't letting her go, not for anything.

"It's okay, sweetheart, I got you now," he murmured as he carried her out of this cabin that had nearly claimed her life twice now. '

Outside, he sank down onto the ground, unable to walk any further, and set Mia on his lap. His cousin Levi approached, and Julian tightened his hold, not ready to part with her yet.

"It's okay, Julian, you can hold her while I examine her," Levi said, anger darkening his features as he took in Mia's bloody body. His eyes were turbulent but his voice gentle when he spoke to Mia. "Hey, honey, first thing I'm going to do is give you a shot of morphine and a sedative, okay? That way you can get some rest while I check out these cuts."

Mia gave what might have been a nod and didn't protest when Levi picked up one of her arms and set up an IV. Head injury, gunshot wound, blood loss, and psychological trauma. When Levi injected the drugs, Mia's eyes fluttered and immediately drifted closed, her injured and exhausted body relaxing against him as she passed out.

"How bad is she, Levi?" he demanded.

"You should have let one of the others carry her," Levi said as he set about cleaning away some of the blood drenching Mia's skin so he could see the cuts.

Since his cousin ignored his question, Julian took that to mean that Mia was in bad shape. "There's so much blood."

"She might need a transfusion," Levi agreed.

"She has a lump on her head."

"Eileen probably knocked her out in the forest to subdue her," Levi said as he started to apply pressure bandages to the wounds on her chest.

"She's going to be okay, though, isn't she?" Julian asked the question he feared hearing the answer to.

"None of these cuts look life-threatening, neither does the bullet hole, the culmination of them has caused substantial blood loss, but she's not bleeding out. These cuts are going to leave horrific scars, and being stalked and nearly killed twice could prove too much for her to handle psychologically. So, in answer to your question, she's not going to die, but she's not okay." Levi paused to meet his gaze directly. "You going to bale on her this time?"

"Nothing on earth could tear me away from her."

Levi smiled. "Then she'll be okay. With time and love and support from her family and friends she'll make it through this."

Mia had that. She had his undying love and support, she had him, all of him, and Julian prayed that would be enough to help her heal.

# OCTOBER 13TH

Mia stared out the hospital window, not really looking at anything.

They'd kept her sedated through most of the night and she'd slept reasonably well without any nightmares.

Julian had been there when she'd finally woken up, but she wasn't ready to talk to him yet so she'd feigned sleep until Levi had come in to examine her.

He was talking to her now, but she wasn't listening. She didn't really care what he had to say about the dozens of cuts marring her skin, Mia felt oddly numb.

Different than how she had felt after surviving Joshua's assault.

Then she'd been scared, angry, hurting, but now she felt … nothing.

It was like she had been encased in concrete and then dropped into the ocean, her body and her mind were sluggish, and she felt heavy—weighed down—it was like she was empty inside.

"Mia."

The sharp command penetrated the fog surrounding her, and she forced her gaze to turn from the window to meet Levi's concerned hazel eyes.

Not knowing what he wanted from her, she just sat and waited for him to say whatever was on his mind.

"I've got you on a high dose of antibiotics because I'm worried about a couple of your wounds, but the blood transfusion last night seemed to help stabilize you. If you remain stable I can discharge you later today," Levi said, speaking slowly and clearly as though he thought she was having trouble understanding him.

She wasn't.

She could hear what he was saying she just didn't care.

Did it really matter?

Infection or no infection, going home today or tomorrow, none of it seemed important.

"Honey, I'm also going to call psych to come and talk to you, okay?" Levi asked tentatively.

He was standing beside her bed checking on her stitches. Mia just stared at him. He could call psych if he wanted to, but what was there to talk about? She had been stalked twice, abducted twice, Julian had been shot and nearly died because of her, and all those children would never be the same because of what Eileen Glass had done to them. And it was all because of her.

No amount of talking in the world could change that.

When she didn't say anything, Levi's concern obviously ramped up, but his voice was calm when he said, "Okay, I'll let you get some more rest. I'll send Julian back in."

"No," the word burst out without any conscious thought.

Now that it was out she realized it was true.

She didn't want Julian to see her like this.

She didn't want *anyone* to see her like this.

In addition to the lump on the side of her head and the gunshot in her arm, her body was a mass of cuts. There were some on her arms and a couple on her legs, but her breasts had taken the brunt of Eileen's anger. They were ugly, red, and enflamed with dozens of little stitches lined up like little soldiers. While the cuts would heal she would be left with horrible scars.

A permanent reminder of what had happened.

"He's been by your side all night, honey, he ..."

"I don't want to see anyone, Levi," she interrupted him. "No one. Please ask the nurses to make sure that no one comes into my room."

With that, she returned her attention to the window. It was gray out, she was on the third floor, and from this angle all she could see was the clouds. If she wasn't so tired she would be figuring out a way to get out of River's End so she never had to see anyone again.

Levi sighed but taped a bandage over the last of her wounds, then he stood and left the room, and she clenched her hands into fists, wondering if he was going to do as she asked or defy her wishes believing he knew what was best for her. Although she could hear hushed voices arguing, her door didn't open again, and she relaxed back against the mattress. Maybe she should ask the next nurse to come in to send in a different doctor. Levi was Julian's cousin so his loyalties lay with him not with her.

Not that she deserved loyalty.

Not after how many lives had been destroyed because of her.

Exhaustion claimed her, and she soon drifted off to sleep.

Pain found her even in sleep as she felt the sharp blade of the knife slice through her flesh over and over again until she fell into a million parts.

Mia woke with a gasp when a hand picked up hers, holding it tightly. The hand was familiar and instantly soothed her in a way that nothing else could.

Opening her eyes, she looked up into her father's smiling face.

That was all it took for the dam to break and then she was sobbing in her father's arm. Each harsh intake of air hurt the gashes on her chest, but she couldn't stop crying if someone held a gun to her head and ordered her to.

"Shh, sweetheart, it's okay, you're okay. Daddy's got you, baby girl." Her father continued with a stream of consolations in that calm, soothing voice he had used when she was a little girl and scared of the monster under the stairs and the one hiding in the closet. Just as it had back then, it slowly eased the noose of terror that was choking her, and eventually, her tears ceased and she lay in his arms, shaking and wishing that he had the power to banish the monsters that haunted her now like he had the ones that scared her as a child.

"I don't want you to leave me," she whispered.

"I'm not going anywhere."

"You are." Tears threatened to burst out again, but she held them back because she didn't want to upset her dad any more than she already had.

"I might have to leave this world, Mia, but I will never leave you, I will always be in your heart, and I will always be watching over you."

"It won't be the same."

"Nothing stays the same forever."

Wasn't that the truth.

Just when she thought she had finally got her life back after Joshua nearly destroyed it someone else came along and shattered the barely dry pieces, breaking them into even smaller ones this time. Pieces that were too small to glue back together.

She didn't know how to get past what Eileen had done.

Didn't think she had the strength left to even try.

Eileen might have been taunting her, but when the woman had said that Julian would never be able to look at her the same way again she hadn't been wrong.

How could he look at her the same way?

Not only was she physically a mess but emotionally as well, and then there were all the people who had been hurt because of her.

"What's going on in that beautiful head of yours, baby girl?" her dad asked as he sat beside her. His hands cupped both of her cheeks, and he leaned in and touched a kiss to her forehead, just beside the lump on her temple. "Julian said you told Levi you didn't want to see him."

"Did Julian call you, tell you to come?"

"No, sweetheart, I've been here ever since they brought you here yesterday afternoon, but I let your man be the one to sit by your side."

"He's not my man," she protested woodenly.

"He loves you," her dad reminded her.

"He *used* to," she corrected, glancing down at her chest. It was covered in bandages beneath her hospital gown, but she remembered the sight of it streaked with her blood. The sight of the knife piercing her skin, the pain, the fear, she remembered every horrible second, and she knew those memories would haunt her for the rest of her days. How could she ask Julian to go through that with her all over again?

"Sweet girl, if you don't know by now that man loves you unconditionally then I've failed you."

"You failed me?" she asked, confused.

"Sweetheart, the kind of love I felt for your mom was all-consuming. It was something I knew I would only find once in my lifetime. You and Julian have that same kind of love. Are you really going to throw that away when you need it the most?" He reached out and brushed a stray lock of hair off her cheek, tucking it behind her ear. "When I die, I want to know you're not alone. I want to know that you have the love and support of a man who loves you more than life itself. I want to know you're going to be okay."

"What Joshua did tore us apart," she reminded her dad. She wasn't sure that the love she and Julian had was the same as what her parents had shared. When times had gotten tough their love had crumbled. "All I'm doing is saving us the pain and heartache of drawing things out."

"No, you're being a coward. You're afraid that you aren't strong enough to survive so you're going to run away and hide, push him away before he can leave. Haven't you learned yet, sweetie? That man never really left you, you two had bumps in the road, big bumps, but neither of you was able to move on because deep down you knew it could never really be over between you. Mia, I'm begging you, don't push him away now, you need him, and … he needs you. He's broken up out there, sweetheart. Not being able to be here for you is killing him."

Understanding hit her like a ton of bricks.

She was doing it again.

The same thing that had come between them last time.

She was ignoring his needs and thinking only about her own. She was feeling guilty and unworthy, ugly and broken, and she was pushing Julian away because it was easier than being afraid that he would look at her and see the same things she felt and leave on his own.

Wrapping her arms around her father's neck, she clung to him. This might be the last time he would be here to offer his support, and she wanted him to know how grateful she was that he was always there for her.

Always.

Without question.

Her trust in her father was unbreakable.

Question was, could she give that same trust to Julian?

\* \* \* \* \*

2:50 P.M.

Julian paced anxiously outside Mia's hospital room, desperate to get in there and make her talk to him. She was shutting him out, wouldn't even let him in the room, and he itched to sit down and find out what was going through her head right now.

If she believed a word that Eileen had said about him never being able to look at her the same way again then he was going to wring her pretty little neck.

Okay, so he wasn't actually going to do that, but she had to know that he would think she was the most gorgeous creature he had ever seen regardless of a few scars on her chest.

Didn't she?

Was that really what Mia was thinking, that she was ugly now?

No, she wasn't wrapped up in her looks, she was beautiful but she never usually bothered with a whole lot of makeup or anything. She was confident in her appearance, she wouldn't be this freaked out about some cuts.

It had to run deeper than that.

The physical scars were a symbol for her psychological scars. His Mia was sweet, caring, compassionate, the kind of person who would rather go hungry herself than let someone else go without. She'd be upset about the others, those kids and him, blaming herself for them being hurt.

Julian was about to go barging into Mia's room and set her straight when the door opened and her father came out.

Before he could even open his mouth and demand to know if Mia was okay the older man smiled at him. "She'll see you now."

Relief actually made him stagger, and he put a hand against the wall to steady himself. "Is she okay?"

"No," Mia's father replied simply. "But you love her, and you'll help her get through this."

"I want to make this better for her," he said, frustrated that this was a problem he couldn't fix.

"I know you do, and so does she, but don't try to fix this for her, just be there to support her."

He nodded, knowing her father was right. Trying to force her to do things his way hadn't worked last time and those that didn't learn from their mistakes were doomed to repeat them.

That wasn't happening.

He wasn't losing her again.

"Mr. Taylor, can you call everyone, ask them to come down

here?"

"You got something in mind?"

"Yeah, but I don't want to say anything till I talk to Mia."

"Is it going to make her smile or cry?" The protective father watched him carefully, and Julian knew that dying or not, Bud Taylor wouldn't hesitate to knock him down if he even so much as caused Mia one speck of pain.

"Hopefully smile."

"Go see your girl, and I'll make the calls."

With a last smile at Mia's father, he walked into her room, relieved when Mia turned from the window and gave him a tentative smile.

Walking straight over to the bed, he perched on the side of it, gently eased an arm around Mia's back, and pulled her into his arms, as mindful as he could be of her cuts and the amount of pain she must be in. Julian buried his face in the crook of her neck and didn't bother to hold back his tears.

He'd nearly lost her.

Come so close he could feel it.

And then having her tell his cousin not to let him come back into the room had tipped him over the edge.

Mia cried along with him, her hands curled into his sweater. "I'm sorry, I'm sorry, I'm sorry," she babbled over and over again.

"Shh, honey, don't be sorry," he said, tightening his hold on her. "I never want you to be sorry for your emotions, but please, sweetheart, don't ever shut me out."

"I won't, I promise I won't do it again."

Julian tried to ease her back so he could see her, but she pressed her face more firmly against his shoulder. "Tell me what's running through that beautiful head of yours."

"I feel guilty, I feel ugly, I feel … empty," she whispered in a tortured voice that cut him to shreds.

He wanted to tell her that she had nothing to feel guilty about, she hadn't done anything wrong. He wanted to tell her that she would always be beautiful to him, but that wouldn't change the fact that she would be left with scars. He wanted to tell her that his love could fill her up, but she had to come to that realization on her own.

Instead, he just nuzzled her neck. "I love you, Mia. I'm here for you, and I'm not walking away from you ever again. I'll hold you in my arms when you're scared, I'll kiss your scars until you believe that they don't change how I see you, I'll do anything you tell me that you need from me. Mia, you're my everything and we *will* get through this."

She lifted her head, and he met her eyes, holding her gaze so that she knew he meant every word he'd said. Something sparked in her eyes, and he knew that his words had gone a small way to easing the emptiness she felt.

Leaning in, he whispered his lips across hers in a feather-light kiss.

With trembling fingers, Mia undid the buttons of his shirt, frowning when she saw the bandage taped to his chest. Her fingers traced around the edges of the bandage. "She shot you."

"But I'm okay," he reminded her. "The bullet bounced off my ribs."

One side of her mouth quirked up. "So you have a hard chest as well as a hard head."

There was his girl.

Her resilience amazed him, and his respect for her grew. She was stronger than she realized, but in time, she would accept that and come to terms with the trauma Eileen Glass had caused her and others in River's End.

But it was over now, and that meant it was time for new beginnings.

"Let's renew our vows," he blurted out before he could talk himself out of it. They both had a lot of physical and psychological healing to do, but he had a feeling that this was an important first step.

"That sounds lovely," Mia said with a smile. "We should plan something really special, maybe around Christmas, with the snow and the decorations, and that Christmassy spirit, it would be the perfect time to get married again, as long as we don't interfere with Theo and Maggie's wedding."

"Uh, honey, I meant now."

"Now? Not right now?"

"Yes, right now as in today."

"Today?" Mia looked down at herself and then gently covered the bandage on his chest with her palm. "You do know that I'm in the hospital, that I have almost two dozen cuts, most of them had to be stitched, and you got shot yesterday."

"I know, and none of it matters."

"But ..."

He silenced her with a fingertip to her lips. "No buts, Mia-bug, I love you, and I hope my baby is growing inside you right now, but if it's not, it will be soon. I want us to be able to start fresh, with nothing between us this time, I want us to have everything that we've ever wanted, and I don't want to wait. I love you."

Mia's eyes grew watery. "And I love you too."

"So, is that a yes?"

She laughed, then kissed him. "Yes, it's a yes."

Julian captured her mouth again, kissing her with more restraint than he wanted in deference to her injuries. "I'll go get everyone."

"Get everyone?"

"I asked your dad to call around and gather the troops. I'm sure they all dropped what they were doing to come rushing over. This might not be as fancy as when we were married for real, but I love you even more today than I did then, and I want all our family and friends here when I commit my life to you all over again."

"Is my dad going to do the ceremony?"

"I hope so, I didn't ask him because I wanted to wait until I asked you first."

"He will. He told me I had to not shut you out again, that you loved me and would never hurt me on purpose. He said I was a coward if I didn't let you in, not into the room but into my soul."

"I knew I loved your dad," he said with a grin. "Should I go let them in?"

"Oh, yeah."

Julian opened the door and found his father, his aunt and uncle, his brother and Renee, his cousins and their women along with baby Dawn, Poppy and Beau, Fletcher, and Mia's father all hanging around in the hall. Everyone he loved there to support them as he and Mia restarted their lives together. Well, almost everyone. They still needed to convince his youngest cousin Dahlia to come back home, but the more time went by, the more that seemed unlikely to ever happen. Despite a very brief visit when Dawn was born, she hadn't been back to River's End in five years.

"Mr. Taylor, Mia and I would love it if you would marry us again," he announced.

Mia's father grinned, and everyone whooped and cheered. There were a few muttered 'about time's' and everyone piled into the small hospital room after him.

"I take it you two are going to say your own vows," Mr. Taylor said.

"Yep," Julian replied. They had last time, and he wanted to this time as well. "You go first," he told Mia.

She reached out her hand and he took it and resumed his place on the bed beside her. "When I first said my vows almost a decade ago, I thought I knew what love was, but I was wrong. Love is doing what's best for the other person even when it hurts you, and love is always putting them first even when they make it hard. Love is never giving up on someone. Julian, you've shown me all of this, and it makes me so grateful that this is where I lived, that this is where you lived, that we were able to meet and fall in love. I haven't always loved you the same way you loved me. When I was suffering, I put myself first and forgot about your needs, but I promise I won't ever do that again. You mean everything to me and I want to spend the rest of my life showing you that. I love you more than I can ever express."

Leaning down, he kissed her hard. "Mia, you think that you didn't put me first, but you got up every morning even though your life was ripped apart, you didn't give up, you fought to climb out of the hole that you'd been tossed into, and that inspired me to be a better man, a better husband, a better lover, a better friend. It inspired me to be the best I could be because I wanted to be worthy of you. Living without you isn't really living, it's just existing, and I don't ever want to experience that again. I'll love you until my dying breath and then into whatever lies beyond this earth. I'd kill for you, I'd die for you, in a heartbeat, without a second thought, but I'd also live for you. You and I belong together, and I won't ever allow anything to come between us again. I love you, Mia-bug."

"I now pronounce you husband and wife again," Mr. Taylor announced, and cheers echoed around the room.

Julian let them fade into the background as he curled an arm around his wife and kissed her, infusing every drop of love he felt for her into that one kiss until he knew for sure that the bond he and Mia shared was stronger than anything life could throw at them.

Jane Blythe is a USA Today bestselling author of romantic suspense and military romance full of sweet, smart, sexy heroes and strong heroines! When she's not weaving hard to unravel mysteries she loves to read, bake, go to the beach, build snowmen, and watch Disney movies. She has two adorable Dalmatians, is obsessed with Christmas, owns 200+ teddy bears, and loves to travel!

To connect and keep up to date please visit any of the following

Amazon – http://www.amazon.com/author/janeblythe
BookBub – https://www.bookbub.com/authors/jane-blythe
Email – mailto:janeblytheauthor@gmail.com
Facebook – http://www.facebook.com/janeblytheauthor
Goodreads – http://www.goodreads.com/author/show/6574160.Jane_Blythe
Instagram – http://www.instagram.com/jane_blythe_author
Reader Group – http://www.facebook.com/groups/janeskillersweethearts
Twitter – http://www.twitter.com/jblytheauthor
Website – http://www.janeblythe.com.au

*sic enim dilexit Deus mundum ut Filium suum unigenitum daret ut omnis qui credit in eum habeat vitam aeternam*